# THE CHRISTMAS BRIDE

~

A Chance Sisters Novella

ANNE GRACIE

"Gracie continues the charming seasonal saga of the four Chance sisters . . . with this thoughtful and tender Regency."

—*Publishers Weekly*

"Exquisitely written, perfectly plotted."

—*Library Journal* (Starred review)

### *The Spring Bride*

"An enchanting spin on Regency tropes with the romance of pragmatic Jane Chance and dashing, disguised gentleman Zachary Black."

—*Publishers Weekly*

"Anne Gracie channels Jane Austen, Georgette Heyer, and fairy tales, most obviously Cinderella…and the result is an enchanting story in which the hero and heroine save one another…I ended the story with a lump in my throat, a smile on my face, and another Anne Gracie keeper in my hand."

—*Heroes and Heartbreakers*

"The main characters are vibrant and complex… the author's skill as a storyteller makes this well worth reading."

—*Kirkus Review*

### *The Summer Bride*

"If you love historical romance that moves you to tears and laughter and introduces you to characters that linger in your memory and in your heart, I suggest you add The Summer Bride to your TBR list ASAP. I plan on rereading all the Chance Sisters books while I wait to see what Anne Gracie has for us next."

—5 stars, Janga, (*The Romance Dish*)

"What fun I had reading The Summer Bride! . . . I hated to put this book down for even a second. . . . You can't go wrong with Anne Gracie's witty writing and with the strong, entertaining plot she created."

—*Harlequin Junkie*

## The Christmas Bride

10 9 8 7 6 5 4 3 2

Printed in the USA.

# Thanks and Acknowledgements

Self publishing is a new venture for me with a whole new learning curve. Thank you to the following friends for their help and encouragement: Carol Marinelli, Kelly Hunter, Fay Thomev, Alison Reynolds, Merilyn Bourke, Pat Rice and Mary Jo Putney and to Keri Arthur for advice, encouragement and for offering to format the book for me.

Dear Reader,

I've received so many lovely emails from readers, asking for a story for Blake Ashton, from *The Autumn Bride*. Thank you so much. I really appreciate your interest and support.

When I first started writing *The Chance Sisters* series I had in mind four 'sisters-of-the-heart' marrying four friends/brothers in arms, or in this case in a trading partnership of four.

I'd intended Ash for Jane, only by the time I came to write Jane's story, I knew her better and I realized she needed a different kind of hero. So Ash got left behind in the Far East—which suited him perfectly. He planned never to return to England.

However, as we all know, to quote the Scots poet Robbie Burns, "The best laid schemes o' mice an' men gang aft a-gley."

For all those lovely people who wrote to me, this story is especially for you.

I hope you enjoy it.

If you've never read any of the *The Chance Sisters* books, this novella is a stand-alone and I've done my best to avoid spoilers, so it won't interfere with your reading pleasure.

Wishing you peace and love and joy for all seasons.

*Anne*

## Chapter One

*England, 1816*

Blake Ashton bent his head against the driving sleet and rode on into the night. He was in a filthy mood. It was clear that fate didn't want him to return to England. Fine by him; he'd never planned to show his face in England again. Ever.

But Max Davenham and Patrick Flynn, his partners in their company, Flynn and Co. Oriental Trading, had called a business meeting for the end of October—in England, damn their eyes, instead of some warm and balmy location in the Far East, where they'd all lived for the last ten years.

The choice of location infuriated him—they knew how he felt about going to England—and why—but he'd been outvoted. So he'd come. Or tried to.

Everything that could go wrong had gone wrong.

First the ship had been becalmed for more than a week, then they were lashed by wild storms that had smashed the main mast and blown them hundreds of miles off course.

They'd ended up stranded on a remote island, and it had taken all of Ash's persuasive abilities— and a show of arms—to get the local people to help them instead of stripping the ship and stealing all it contained. He'd written to let his partners know he was alive, but added that since he'd missed the date of the meeting, there was no point in continuing to England.

So he'd given up and gone back home—or at least what had passed for home at the time. He was a rolling stone, and gathered no moss, moving from place to place and country to country as the whim took him. The world was his oyster, he told himself.

Max's reply had flicked him on the raw. Max made it clear that he believed that Ash had had no intention of coming to England in the first place and had found the delay quite convenient.

The fact that it was true had Ash gritting his teeth, and when he received a letter from his other partner, Flynn, saying much the same—and with no subtlety at all—telling him to *grasp the nettle once and for all and get over your funk, lad!* Ash made up his mind. He'd damned well show them he wasn't afraid—or ashamed—to come home.

Not that England was his home any more. Home was just a word.

He'd finally landed in England in early December. He'd made straight for the company's London office, only to find that Max and Flynn—and Freddy Monkton-Coombes, their fourth silent partner—had all gone down to Davenham Hall in Devon for Christmas. For a *family* Christmas, curse them.

It was almost the last straw. Ash wanted to turn around and sail back out to sea. But he wasn't going to let them think him a coward. He'd show his face, then leave.

However the deeper into England he travelled the clearer it became that the fates were still against him. He'd hired a post chaise, but the further west they traveled the worse the weather and the roads became. Then, traveling on a surface churned into a slippery morass of half-frozen mud, the postilion had mistaken the road in the darkness and they'd ended up in a ditch with a broken axle.

They'd walked to the next village and, when he found he was only about fifteen miles from Davenham Hall and there was no other equipage available, Ash had hired a horse to ride the last few miles. He left the postilion to oversee the carriage repairs and transport the rest of his baggage to Davenham Hall when that was done.

He pressed on. It started snowing again, not the soft, gentle floating flakes of white that he remembered from childhood, but hard, sleety pellets of ice that stung his face. His mood worsened.

Rounding a bend on the edge of a thicket of trees he came across fallen branches strewn across the road, blocking his way. He swore and slowed his horse to a walk, narrowing his eyes against the darkness, looking for a pathway around the blockage.

"Stand and deliver!" The voice rang out. A short man in a long coat stepped forward. He was muffled to the eyes with his hat pulled low. "Throw down your valuables." His voice was hoarse. His pistol showed in brief silhouette against the snowy background.

Ash was cross, cold, tired and in no mood to be robbed. He pulled out his own pistol.

The footpad's pistol wavered in surprise, but he did not lower his gun. For a moment the two men simply stared at each other.

"I'll wager I'm a better shot than you are," Ash said. "Drop your gun or you die."

The words were barely out of his mouth when a small figure rushed out at him from the other side of the road yelling "No! No! No!"

Ash's horse shied in fright, there was a loud report from the footpad's gun, something stung his cheek, and Ash fired his own pistol in response.

Ash brought his horse back under control. The footpad was a still, dark huddle on the ground, and a small figure was bent over it. "Charley! Charley! Are you dead, Charley?"

A child? Out here in this weather? At this time of night?

"Charleeeeey!" the boy wailed. He turned to Ash, his face a pale shape in the darkness. "You've killed her, you've killed Charley."

*Her?* Ash pocketed his pistol and leapt from his horse.

The boy flung himself at Ash, pummeling him in terror and fury. "Don't you touch her! Don't you dare! You've killed her, you've killed her!"

"Stop that, boy!" He caught the boy's fists in his hands. "Let me look at her—you did say she was a girl, didn't you? Your mother?"

"My sister."

Dear Lord, what the hell was a girl doing, playing footpad? "Let me see. You don't know if she's dead or not. She might have only swooned." He released the boy.

The boy looked to be about eight or nine, skinny and distraught, and dressed in a coat too big for him. "She's bleeding." He held up a small bare hand and even in the gloom, Ash could see the dark stain of blood

"Let me look." Ash thrust the boy to one side, and knelt down in the mud beside the girl's body. He pulled the muffler aside and pressed his fingers to the side of her throat, searching for a pulse. He held his breath and concentrated.

"She's alive. She's breathing." Ash breathed

again. He hadn't meant to kill anyone, let alone a girl. But his hand came away sticky with warm blood. She might die yet.

He pulled off his neckcloth, wadded it up into a pad, tucked it inside the girl's coat and tied it down with her muffler, hoping it might stop, or at least slow, the bleeding. There wasn't enough light to see exactly where she'd been shot.

The sleet started again. "Fetch my horse," he told the boy.

"It's gone. It ran away."

Ash swore silently. "We have to get her to shelter. Where do you live?"

The boy hesitated, his thin little face torn with doubt. "I'm not supposed to tell."

"Do you want your sister to die out here in the cold?" Ash snapped.

"No," the boy said in a very small voice.

"Well then?"

"This way," the child said on a sob, and pointed to what seemed like a thicket of bushes. Ash could barely make out a faint track between them. He scooped the girl into his arms—she weighed about as much as a newborn foal—and followed.

Instead of the town or village Ash had hoped for, there was just one small cottage at the end of a muddy track. Ash stared at the lonely, tumble-down dwelling. There was no sign of life, no light burning inside, not even any smoke from a fire. "Is this where your family lives?"

"Me and Charley, yes."

"What about your parents?"

"Dead."

"Don't you have any neighbors?"

The boy nodded. "The closest is old Mr. Johnston, over that way." He pointed. "But he doesn't like visitors. There's a farm over there"—he gestured in the opposite direction—"but it's a long walk."

"Run ahead and open the door." Ash was breathing heavily. The girl was weighing rather more than a newborn foal by now. The boy ran ahead and pushed open the door. No lock, Ash noticed.

He bent to go through the low doorway. He could barely see in the gloom. The boy tugged at his arm. "The bed's over here."

Ash laid her on it and unbuttoned her greatcoat. But he could barely see her face, let alone tell how bad her injury was. "Candles?"

"Charley made rushlights, but there's nothing to light them with. The fire's out."

"A tinder box?"

The boy ran and fetched the tinder box and a rushlight. It took a few tries before Ash could coax a tiny flame from the tinder. He lit the proffered rushlight. It sputtered a moment, then caught, offering a feeble flame.

He lit another two rushlights and turned back to the girl. Her eyes fluttered and opened. She squinted up at him. 'What—Who are—Toby?"

"I'm here, Charley." The little boy's face was pinched and stained with tears.

"Don't worry," Ash told her. "You've been hurt, but you're going to be all right. I just have to get this off you." He lifted her to slide down the sleeves of the greatcoat and get to her wound. She moaned in pain and fainted again. Taking advantage of her swoon Ash quickly stripped her of the coat, her waistcoat and shirt before she woke again. He was thankful to discover she wore a chemise underneath, tucked into a pair of breeches. But beneath that she was woefully thin.

He examined the wound, and breathed a sigh of relief. It was a flesh wound. His ball had pierced the muscle of her upper arm, but as far as he could tell, hadn't connected with the bone at all. Best of all, it had passed clean through her, which meant he wouldn't have to try to extract the ball.

Of course she wasn't out of danger yet. It might not be a mortal wound, but men had died of smaller injuries. Infection and fever were as much a danger as the wound itself.

"Bring water and clean cloths," he told the boy. Hot water would be best, but with no fire, there was no possibility of that.

The boy carefully lifted a kettle from a hook

in the fireplace and poured water from it into a bowl. The water was lukewarm—so why was the fire not still burning? It was freezing inside the cottage.

Ash cleaned the wound as best he could, making sure no threads of clothing had been pushed into her flesh with the ball. It was hard to tell in the dim light of the rushlights.

He tried to think of what to do next. He'd lived the last ten years in the tropics, where the tiniest cut could fester and a man could die in days.

"Does your sister have anything to treat cuts and scrapes? Any salves? Alcohol of any kind?" Foolish question. The most cursory glance had told him these two had very little.

The boy rummaged in a small chest and brought out a small leather-covered bottle. He offered it to Ash. "Papa's brandy flask." He shook it. "It sloshes."

"Perfect." He unstoppered the flask, and cautiously sniffed to test the contents. The heady aroma of good brandy filled his nostrils. He closed his eyes briefly. He hadn't touched a drop in almost ten years.

Her eyelids fluttered again. She was coming around. Quickly he positioned her arm and carefully dripped brandy into her wound. She recoiled with a scream.

The boy instantly attacked. "Stop it! You're hurting her!" But she'd fainted again.

Ash held him back with one hand "Hush, boy, I know it hurts but it will help prevent any infection. Now help me hold her up. I need to pour brandy into the exit wound before she wakes. It won't hurt her while she's in a swoon."

Doubt etched the boy's thin face, but he helped steady his sister as Ash dripped the last of the brandy into the exit wound.

"Now, get me some clean cloths for a bandage."

The boy shook his head. "We used up the last cloths for cleaning the blood."

"Then fetch me her best petticoat—a clean one, mind."

The boy went back to the small chest, took a folded white petticoat from it and handed it to Ash. It was clean but thin and threadbare and patched in several places. Her best petticoat?

The boy gasped as Ash pulled out his knife, cut the seam, then ripped the first strip off the petticoat. "Charley will blister your ears when she learns what you did."

Ash just hoped she survived to do it. He tore the fabric into strips, made a pad of some and used the rest to bind it to her wound. He settled her back on the bed, tugged off her boots, and after brief hesitation, slid the damp and muddy breeches off her, trying not to notice the long, slender legs they'd covered. He tucked the bedclothes around her, noting how thin and inadequate they seemed, and for the first time, took a good look at the woman he'd shot.

She was young, though not as young as he'd feared, given the boy's age. She looked to be about nineteen or twenty, fine-featured and pretty, with a heart-shaped face, smooth, pale skin, a lush-looking mouth and a straight little nose. Her lashes were long and thick, dark crescents against the pallor of her skin. Her hair was sable dark and glossy, pulled back into a tight knot that had started to come loose. He felt for the pins that held it in place and pulled them out. Soft curls fell, clustering around her face.

Ash smoothed them back. She looked young and delicate and vulnerable. What the hell was she doing holding up travelers at gunpoint?

## Chapter Two

The small, one-roomed cottage was clean and neat, but that was the best Ash could say about it. The bed was not much more than a wide shelf in a corner alcove, with a mattress stuffed with straw, and couple of faded, mismatched curtains strung across for privacy.

Apart from that there was a small table and a couple of rickety-looking chairs. A few pots and pans hung on the wall and some mismatched crockery sat on a shelf. A line of books sat on another shelf. No rugs on the hard stone floor, just a couple of old sacks. A fireplace was set into one wall, black and empty but for a small pile of dead-looking coals.

No wonder the place was freezing.

"Right, let's get that fire going," Ash said to the boy, who was hovering, white-faced and anxious. "Toby, is it? Where do you keep the wood? In this?" A large basket sat on the floor near the fire, an old sack thrown over it. Ash reached for it, then recoiled in surprise as a large brown duck reared its head at him with a loud "Quack!"

Toby leaped forward, seizing the duck in a protective embrace. "Don't hurt her! It's Hannibelle. She's mine."

"Annabelle? You keep a duck called Annabelle inside the house?"

"No, her name is Hannibelle — with an *H*."

"Annabelle with an *H*?"

The boy clutched the duck tighter. "When I first got her I thought she was a boy, and quite adventurous, so I called her Hannibal." At Ash's blank look, he added, "You know, Hannibal, the general who crossed The Alps with elephants."

Ash nodded. He knew who Hannibal was, but he wouldn't expect a boy from a tumbledown slum to know the name of an ancient Carthaginian general, let alone name a duck after him. He glanced at the line of books. Run-down cottages didn't usually contain books of any kind, let alone a shelf of them.

And now he came to think about it, this boy didn't speak with any kind of rural country accent, but clear, unaccented, educated English of the sort that Ash himself spoke.

"She was wounded—some hunters shot her and she can't fly. But Charley made her better and we decided to keep her. Only then she laid an egg, so we changed her name to Hannibelle — with an *H*." He put the duck back in her basket, adding, "She sleeps inside at night. Because of foxes."

"I see. So how do you know about Hannibal the general?"

The boy rolled his eyes. "Charley is teaching me stuff. She says I'll need it when I go away to school."

Ash nodded. "You will indeed." There was a mystery here. A gently raised boy and his sister, without any visible means of support, in a ramshackle cottage in the middle of nowhere. A sister who dressed as a man and held up travelers at night—presumably because she was desperate—and who by day, educated her brother in ancient history.

But first things first. "Where's the wood then, since it's not kept in Hannibelle's basket?"

Toby showed him a ragged pile of wood stacked at the back door. Another basket sat beside it, filled with what looked like . . .

"Cows' plop," Toby said matter-of-factly. "We collect it when it's dry and burn it. It's easier to get than wood." He saw Ash's expression and laughed. "I know it sounds horrid, but it's not too bad, really. Better than being cold."

Ash supposed so. After ten years in the warmer climes of the Far East he was finding the English winter bitter. And it was only December, with the colder weather still to come. Lord knew how these two managed.

He collected some wood, and set a fire. There

was no spare paper in the cottage so he pulled out the knife he carried in his boot and shaved off some curls of wood for kindling. Toby handed him some twisted strands of dried grass. "Charley uses these, too." He eyed Ash's knife enviously. "I'm not allowed to have a knife yet, not until I'm twelve Charley says."

The rushlights had burned out, so Ash used the tinder box again and soon he had a small fire burning. He piled on the wood.

"That's a lot of wood," Toby said doubtfully. "We have to be careful. Winter is long and we don't want to run out." He was clearly repeating what he'd been told.

"Don't worry," Ash said. "I'll replace anything we burn."

Once the fire was burning brightly he lit another few rushlights and checked the girl. She was awake, her eyes big and dark and wary. In the shadowy corner, he couldn't tell what color they were.

"Who are you?"

"Blake Ashton, at your service." He bowed slightly.

"You shot me."

"Yes, I'm sorry about that. I didn't mean to. Something startled my horse."

There was small sound behind him, and Toby said, "I'm sorry Charley. It was my fault. I threw stones at him. And yelled. I thought he was going to kill you."

"I told you to stay inside, Toby," she whispered.

"I know. I'm sorry. But I was scared."

The boy was right to be scared, Ash thought. What if she'd held up someone else? Another traveller might have shot her without a thought and ridden on. She would have bled out in the snow with nobody the wiser.

On the other hand, if the boy hadn't startled his horse, would Ash have shot at all? He'd never know.

She looked at Ash. "What are you going to do?"

"Stay here until morning, then see what our options are."

"Stay here? You can't—" She tried to sit up, then moaned.

"Stop that. You'll hurt yourself."

She glared at him. "You already did that."

"And you shot at me."

"Not to hit you," she said indignantly. "I fired over your head. Just to let you know I was serious."

Ash shook his head. Females and guns. "You're lucky I didn't kill you. You shouldn't be firing a pistol at all. What the devil did you think you were doing?"

Her expression turned mutinous. "None of your business," she muttered and turned her head away.

"Seeing as I'm stuck here for the night, it is my business."

"What do you mean stuck here?"

"My horse bolted. I'm without transport, and it's sleeting." He glanced at the window. "Actually I think it's now turned to snow." He shivered. "Ghastly climate."

"It's winter, what do you expect? Anyway, you can't stay here."

"I'm not going anywhere. Now, with Toby's help I will get us all something to eat, and we'll settle in for the night."

Her eyes narrowed and she stiffened. "Don't you dare—Toby, where's Papa's pistol?"

"I've got it here, Charley. You dropped it and I—"

"My dear girl, rid yourself of the notion that I have any base designs on your virtue, such as it may be. You're wounded, and I don't, er,"—he glanced at the boy anxiously clutching what looked like a fine dueling pistol—"*dally* with wounded—or unwilling—females. Besides, you have Toby and Hannibelle as chaperones."

"You've met Hannibelle?"

"I have. Now, get it out of your head that I mean you or your brother or his duck any harm—any further harm, I mean. My word as a gentleman on it, so stop fussing and try to sleep."

Reluctantly she lay back down, but her eyes remained open, burning dark with suspicion in her unnaturally pale face.

He had to give it to her—her arm must be hurting like the very devil, but she was making no complaint.

Ash turned to the task of making dinner. He hadn't always been rich, with servants to see to his every need, and he knew the rudiments of cooking. But cooking a meal here was no simple matter. There seemed to be very little food in the house; a bag of dried beans, a bag of rolled oats, some dried greens, and the hard heel that was all that remained of a loaf of bread.

Hanging on a hook beside the fireplace he found a covered pot of beans. He stirred them. They were soft and almost cooked. He tasted them and made a face. Bland and floury. He investigated the dried greens. Some kind of herb. He tossed them into the pot, stirred them in well and transferred the pot to the hook over the fire.

"I don't suppose there's any spices, or even any meat," he commented, not expecting any answer. "These beans are crying out for some flavor." For the last decade he'd been used to the spicy foods of the Far East, and it was hard to get used to the bland fare he'd been served in England. Let alone this bean mush.

To his surprise, Toby sprang defensively to his

feet, fists clenched. "You're not going to cook my Hannibelle!"

"Settle down, boy, I had no intention of thrusting your pet into the pot."

Toby glanced at his sister. "Charley said once that if things don't improve we might have to eat Hannibelle. But I won't, I won't. She's my friend."

"There, there, nobody's going to eat your duck. My word on it," Ash said soothingly.

He was starting to think maybe it had turned out for the best, being accosted by an incompetent footpad and her little brother. These two were in a desperate situation, and though he told himself he was not responsible, he could easily ensure they weren't driven to such perilous lengths again.

He glanced at the still figure in the bed and saw the long lashes flutter. As long as she survived the next few days.

The beans were hot enough, so he served them up. It was a disgusting mess of a meal and Ash ate sparingly. The boy ate with a telling appetite. Hunger was the best spice.

He checked on the sister. Exhaustion and injury had finally defeated fear and suspicion, and she was sound asleep.

"So, Charley, that's short for . . ?"

"Charlotte." The boy scraped his bowl clean.

"And you are. . ?"

"Oh sorry." The boy rose and gave a quick bow.

"Toby, sir, Tobias Underwood."

"And I'm Blake Ashton." The boy didn't learn those manners in a cottage.

Toby finished his food and went to collect the bowls. Ash's was half full. "Don't you want this?"

"No, I ate earlier," Ash lied.

"Mind if I finish it off? Charley says we can't afford to waste food."

"Go ahead." As the boy polished off his bean mush, Ash asked casually, "So how long have you and your sister lived here?"

"Just this year—since the spring." Toby wrinkled his nose. "It's not very nice, is it? Home is much nicer, but we can't go back there until Charley turns twenty-one."

"And why is that?"

"That's enough, Toby," a voice rasped from the bed alcove. "Don't bother the gentleman with our private concerns."

Ash hurried over to the bed. "How are you feeling, Miss Underwood?"

To his surprise she looked at her brother and said in a long-suffering way, "Toby."

"I'm sorry, Charley, I forgot." The boy immediately turned to Ash and said, "Sorry sir, I forgot. My name is Toby *Smith*, and my sister is Miss Charlotte *Smith*.

The girl closed her eyes with a sigh.

"Of course it is." Ash kept a straight face. "A

mistake anyone could make. Now, if you'll wash those dishes, Toby, I'll have a little chat to your sister."

Toby nodded and started clattering away, and Ash turned back to the girl. "How are you feeling Miss *Smith*?"

She gave him a hostile glance, tried to move and winced. "Wonderful."

In a soft voice that he hoped the boy wouldn't hear, he said, "You need not worry about the boy's slip with the name. I've been out of England for almost ten years, and there's nobody I would know to tell—even if I were the sort to gossip, which I'm not. But while it's none of my business why you and your brother are hiding out in a freezing hovel, in obviously dire straits, holding people up on the road—"

"You were the first."

"Thank God for that. So there's nobody pursuing you?" A flicker of expression in her eyes caused him to add, "Somebody *is* pursuing you?"

"I've done nothing wrong. Apart from . . . you."

"That wasn't what I asked."

Her expression turned mulish.

"Very well, keep your secrets. I have no interest in them. I don't suppose you're hungry. There is some bean mus—bean stew if you'd like it."

She shook her head and closed her eyes. In pain, he thought. "Do you have anything for the pain?"

he asked. "Something tucked away, for safety?"

"There's some brandy—"

"I used it to clean your wound."

She opened one eye and gave him a suspicious glance.

He held up his hands. "I swear that was all. I don't drink. Haven't touched a drop in almost ten years.

She gave him a doubtful look, then closed her eyes with a sigh, as if it was all too hard. Which it probably was. Ash pulled the covers over her, careful not to bump her wound.

She was very young, too young to be living on her own, supporting herself and a little brother. And a duck. Without much success, going by the conditions she was living in, and the desperate resort to highway robbery. The thought still made him furious. He might have killed her, dammit! And he'd never hurt a female in his life.

Not physically at least. And never deliberately. He forced his thoughts back to the present.

Did they still hang footpads, or might a young and pretty female footpad have her sentence transmuted to transportation instead? Either way, it didn't bear thinking about. Ash hoped it was the truth that he was her first. He was fully resolved to be the last.

So who or what was she hiding from?

The last rushlight guttered. The fire was fading.

He supposed the only alternative to sitting in the dark was to go to bed.

He glanced at the sleeping girl. One bed.

"You sleep with your sister?" he asked Toby.

The boy nodded. "It's warmer."

"Right, well, you slide in first and I'll hop in next to you."

Toby looked doubtful. "But—"

"I'm not sleeping on that cold stone floor. It'll be a squeeze, but it'll be warmer with three."

Toby nodded. "I know. It's not that. It's . . . I . . . ." He looked embarrassed. "I have to get up in the night sometimes, to use the pot."

"Ah." He glanced at the girl and gave a mental shrug. "Very well, I'll take the inside wall and you sleep on the outside and we'll keep Charley warm between us. Get ready while I tend to the fire."

He built up the fire, dredging up half-forgotten memories from the past, trying to remember how to ensure a fire burned slow and steady through the night. Tricky. It was something that servants did. And for the past decade he'd been more interested in staying cool than getting warm.

He turned and found Toby sitting on the edge of the bed without his shoes or jacket. "I'm ready."

"You wear your clothes to bed?"

Toby nodded. "Since the weather got colder, we both do."

Made sense. Ash pulled off his own boots and

removed his greatcoat and coat, both of which were still damp. He draped them over the chairs and hoped they'd be dry by morning. His buckskin breeches too were damp. He unfastened them and eased them off. At least he was wearing drawers.

He gestured to Toby. "You hop in first, I'll climb in after you." Toby slipped in beside his sister, and Ash carefully climbed across them both.

"And close the curtains," Toby whispered.

Ash sighed and reached over them to pull the curtains across.

"Charley usually does it. You haveta be careful, otherwise they—oh."

They both looked at the collapsed curtains.

"That's why you haveta be careful," Toby whispered.

The curtains had been held up by string, not a rail, Ash realized belatedly. "Oh well," he began, intending to leave them there until morning.

"Charley says they help keep us warm."

"Right." Cursing silently Ash clambered back across the sleeping sister and the interestedly watching boy and groped around in the gloom until he found the ends of the string and hooked them back on the nails in the wall. By the time he'd rehung the curtains and closed them to Toby's satisfaction—"Charley says if you leave even a little gap the cold air gets in"—his own feet were frozen.

He climbed back across the sleeping sister, and carefully slipped down between her and the wall. It was a tight fit. The wall was freezing. The sister was not.

Ash frowned. How hot was too hot? He felt her forehead. Warm, but not burning up. He hoped.

He wriggled down and tried to make himself comfortable. With bits of straw sticking into him from the ridiculously thin mattress, only partly covered by the wholly inadequate covers, and caught between a lissome young woman and a freezing wall, Ash figured he'd be lucky if he got any sleep at all.

He folded his arms, closed his eyes and ordered himself to sleep.

## Chapter Three

There was a woman in his arms, soft, willing, her limbs entwined with his. Ash lay for a moment with his eyes closed, enjoying the sense of well-being and warmth and the insistent pleasurable ache of desire.

As his thoughts came slowly together he marveled that he'd slept at all in this damned uncomfortable bed, let alone—

*A woman in his arms!*

His eyes flew open. And found himself face to face with his footpad. She was pressed up against him, half glued to his chest, her thighs wrapped around his, as close and intimate as she could possibly get.

One of his arms was wrapped around her, holding her close. How did they get that way? Had he reached for her in the night? Or had she reached for him?

His thigh had somehow ended up between hers, pressed firmly against her softness. His other hand rested on the gentle swell of her backside.

Her face was bare inches from his. Her breathing was soft, regular. Beneath her eyelids her eyes flickered, as if she were dreaming.

She was sound asleep.

There was no shadow of awareness in her face, not of their relative positions, or of the ... the state of him. He took a deep breath and tried to will his inappropriate arousal away. His exhalation coiled in a smoky cloud before his eyes, and realization dawned.

*Cold.* It was the cold that had caused them to end up like this. Nothing to do with lust or sexual desire. This damned impossible climate.

He carefully released her backside, and slowly eased his thigh out from its intimate, incriminating position.

Not a man and woman seeking comfort from each other, but two cold bodies seeking warmth. Two cold bodies? He looked, and found Toby curled against his sister's back, snuggled deep under the covers for warmth. Three.

It was morning; there was light coming through the threadbare bed-curtains. Time to get up and see what he could do about this impossible position. The situation, he meant.

As for the position ... He didn't move, didn't want to move. He lay quietly, gazing at her in the faint morning light. Her skin was fine like silk, and pale but with a scattering of tiny freckles across the bridge of her nose.

Her mouth . . . No, better not to look or think about her mouth, so pillowy soft and lush and tempting. A mouth for a man to dream about. To wonder what she might taste like.

He watched her breathing. Thick dark lashes shielded eyes that looked faintly bruised. Lack of sleep, and not just one sleepless night. And that lush mouth was set firm, above a chin that had already turned mulish on him more than once.

In sleep she looked young and fragile and vulnerable. He was a cur to have such thoughts about her. He'd *shot* her, for God's sake.

Young? Not yet twenty-one. Old enough to care for a little brother for the better part of a year without any apparent support. Fragile? Fragile didn't dress like a man and take a pistol out on a wintry night to rob a stranger on the highway. And vulnerable? She might be, but she wasn't going to admit it, just as she'd refused to admit that her wound was damnably painful.

Young, desperate, valiant and stubborn.

His money belt—even a fraction of the contents of his money belt—would set these two up in comfort for a year or two. Charlotte and Toby Underwood were not his responsibility. He could just ease himself out of this pathetic excuse for a bed, and creep away, leaving a pile of shining gold coins on the table as a farewell gift.

So easy to slip his boots and coat back on—and

his breeches—find his way back to the road, and walk to Davenham Hall. At a guess it would only be ten miles or so.

And then, back to his life. Have the meeting with Max and Flynn and Freddy, prove to them that he wasn't a coward, that it didn't bother him in the least to return to England, and then . . .

Then back to his life in the Far East. Balmy breezes, azure skies, spicy foods, and warm, willing, golden-skinned, sloe-eyed women.

Leaving quietly was the obvious thing to do. He had no connection to these two, no responsibility—except that he *had* wounded her, his conscience reminded him. But she'd made it clear—more than clear—that she didn't want him here.

But there was no way he could leave an injured woman and a child to fend for themselves.

Even if she hadn't been injured—and by his own hand—she and the boy were in trouble, and though he'd spent a lifetime avoiding other people's troubles, somehow, this time, he couldn't just walk away.

Who was she hiding from and why? She wouldn't tell him, that was clear. But the boy, yes, young Toby had already let several things slip. Ash would talk to Toby.

It wasn't taking advantage of a little boy's trusting nature he told his conscience. It was for their own good.

Ash eased himself out of the bed into the bitter chill of morning. His clothes were cold, so cold he couldn't tell whether they were dry or not. Not that he had any choice. Even inside the cottage his breath came in clouds. How many years since he'd seen his own breath? He dressed quickly and stepped outside in search of the outhouse—and found himself in a world transformed.

Snow lay on the ground in a blanket, thick and deep, along bare, frost-edged branches, a delicate tracery of silver etched in charcoal against a leaden sky. A spider web hung between two bushes, glittering drops of crystal catching the light, prettier and more delicate than any diamond necklace could ever be.

Where was the spider? Could spiders live in this cold? He had no idea.

The freezing air scoured his lungs, almost painful, but invigorating. He stamped his feet to warm them. The sound echoed in the still morning. He couldn't hear any birds. Probably all flown south for the winter. Sensible creatures. He wished he'd done the same.

He returned to the cottage and set about getting the fire going.

"Are you making breakfast?" Toby stood at his elbow. He was fully dressed, but his eyes were full of sleep and his hair stuck up in all directions.

"Fetch a basin and I'll pour some warm water for you to wash in," he told the boy.

As Toby washed, Ash ran his fingers through his own hair and ruefully felt his stubbled jaw. His shaving things were in the saddlebags of the damned horse that had run off last night. He hoped the creature had found shelter.

"Is it porridge again?" Toby asked.

"I don't think we have much choice." It was that or beans. Ash looked at the bag of oats. He'd never made porridge in his life. He poured some into the pot and stirred in some water.

"You forgot the salt," Toby said.

"Salt? In porridge?"

Toby nodded. "Nanny used to make it for me and she always put salt in. It's the Scots way, Nanny said, and they make the best porridge. Nanny is Scottish."

Ash handed the boy a spoon. "You're the expert. You make the porridge then."

"No, we use this." Toby held up a well-used twig. "It's a proper Scottish spurtle."

It looked like an ordinary English twig to Ash, but he wasn't going to make an issue of it. "Excellent. Go ahead then."

So the boy had had a Scottish nanny. The mystery deepened.

While Toby stirred the porridge, Ash checked on the sister. She was still asleep. He smoothed her silky hair back and felt her forehead. Warm. Again, he wasn't sure whether it was too warm or not. He would have liked to check her wound, but sleep was probably better for her at this time. He wished he knew more about treating injuries.

He tucked the bedclothes more securely around her and closed the bed curtains.

The boy carefully served up the porridge into two bowls, leaving some in the pot for his sister. He put a little of his own share aside on a battered tin dish. "For Hannibelle," he explained, catching Ash's curious look. "It needs to cool. Then I'll put her outside for a little while. But not for long. It's too cold for ducks, plus foxes are especially hungry in the winter and she can't fly."

After breakfast Ash went to fetch more firewood and noticed it was running low. "Is there an ax?" he asked Toby.

The boy showed him where it was. "I'm not allowed to chop wood yet. Charley said you have to be twelve."

"That's right," Ash agreed. So she chopped her own wood. Somehow that made him angry. She ought not to be in such a position.

He and the boy dragged in fallen branches from the forest and Ash spent the next hour chopping furiously. It took him a while to get into the swing of it—it was years since he'd chopped wood, and then it was only for fun. But at least he was warm now and the cottage would be easier to keep warm.

He made a stack by the back door, and built up the fire. She was still sleeping. He turned to the boy. "You said last night there was a farm not far away."

Toby slid him a look of mixed anxiety and suspicion. "Why do you want to know?"

"Farms usually have plenty of food. We could buy some from them. Maybe some ham or bacon, cheese, fresh eggs . . . whatever they have."

Toby's eyes widened. "That would cost a fortune."

"Let's see, shall we?"

The farm wasn't very far, Toby assured him. They left Charley sleeping. Ash wasn't sure whether the soundness of her sleep was a good thing or not, but he had no choice but to leave her.

Surprisingly, he enjoyed the walk, freezing as the day was, with a leaden sky that he thought might offer the promise of more snow. Toby showed him the way, hopping along cheerfully, full of observations and questions.

Ash had questions of his own.

"When do you think you'll be able to go back home—your real home, I mean. What was it called again?"

Toby walked along a snow-covered log, balancing carefully. "Old Place, you mean?"

"Yes, when will you go back?" Old Place. The name of a house, not a village.

Toby frowned in concentration, then jumped from the end of one log to another. He slipped and would have fallen, but Ash grabbed him and helped him to rebalance. Toby grinned. "Charley would have blistered my ears for that. She says we can't afford to get hurt or sick." The brightness in his face faded. "She's going to be all right, isn't she, Mr. Ashton?"

"I'll make sure of it," Ash promised. "I'll ask at the farm if there's a doctor we can get to check on her injury."

Toby's face crumpled with anxiety. "I don't think Charley would like that. She says we shouldn't tell people our business."

"Why is that?" Ash asked casually. "Oh look, is that a robin?" He pointed to a small bird watching them curiously from a tangle of twigs.

"Yes, Charley and I feed them sometimes, even though you shouldn't waste food. She's very fond of robins."

"You were going to tell me why Charley doesn't want people to know your business. I suppose that includes me, doesn't it?"

Toby considered that. "I don't know. She worries about people talking but, well, you're not 'people' are you, sir? You're staying with us, and you're helping us, and you're a gentleman, so . . . "

"So if I promise not to tell a soul, and you don't tell Charley what you've told me, she won't be worried, will she?"

Toby brightened. "No, she won't."

"So why aren't you living at Old Place anymore?"

"Papa killed himself—shot himself with a gun—I'm not supposed to know."

"And someone else owns the house now?"

"No, it still belongs to me—I'm the heir—but Cousin Albert is our guardian now and we have to do what he says." He darted a glance at Ash. "I don't like Cousin Albert."

"I see."

The boy walked carefully along another log. "Cousin Albert wants Charley to marry Cousin Eustace Albert—he's Cousin Albert's son."

"And Charley doesn't want to marry Cousin Eustace Albert?"

"No, not at all. Cousin Eustace Albert is a bit strange. His eyes roll around. And he dribbles."

Ash felt a spurt of anger on Charley's behalf. "Your sister doesn't seem like the kind of girl who could be forced to do anything she didn't want."

"No, but Cousin Albert is using me as a pawn."

Ash raised a brow. "Do you know what that means?"

Toby nodded matter-of-factly. "Yes, it's from chess—do you play chess? I do. A pawn is something that doesn't matter except for tactical purposes. Cousin Albert is using me to make Charley do what he wants."

"How is he using you?"

"He says if Charley doesn't marry Cousin Eustace Albert, Cousin Albert will send me to the Grimswade School for Boys."

It didn't sound so bad to Ash. Boys were sent away to school all the time. He'd been sent to Eton when he was about Toby's age. "I've never heard of the Grimswade School for Boys."

"Charley found out about it. She says it's a bad place. It's a charity school and the conditions are terrible—two boys died there last year—and the masters are very cruel. In any case she says when I'm old enough— twelve or so—I'm to go to Papa's old school, Eton. That's why she's teaching me Latin and Greek and stuff."

Ash blinked. "Charley knows Latin and Greek?"

Toby burst into peals of laughter. "Of *course* not, she's *a girl*!" When he'd recovered from this deliciously silly notion, he explained. "But it's all in the books, so Charley says all we have to do is read them and learn. She says the Romans who spoke Latin are dead, so the pronunciation doesn't matter, just the vocabulary and the grammar. Greek is much harder though. They have a different alphabet. Charley is trying to work it out. That and mathematics. I don't think girls are very good at it."

"They can be, if they're taught it," Ash said. "One of the best mathematicians I ever knew was a woman."

Toby gave him a skeptical glance, so Ash told him about Madam Liu, a tiny, wizened old Chinese lady who could add up a column of numbers in the blink of an eye, work out a percentage, and calculate profit and loss in another two blinks, all without resorting to paper, pen or abacus. "And she spotted anomalies in financial accounts the way a musician might spot off notes in a symphony."

Toby's politely bland expression conveyed that he considered distant Chinese mathematical women a poor choice of conversation, so Ash added, "I could help you with mathematics, if you want."

"No thank you," Toby said quickly. "I don't really like lessons. I'd rather learn to shoot." He gave Ash a hopeful look, but Ash had not completely forgotten the wiles of young boys.

"And will Charley teach you that, too?"

Toby screwed up his nose. "Not until I'm twelve, she says."

They walked on for a time, then Ash said casually, "Is there no-one else who you and your sister could live with?"

Toby sighed. "No, because we don't have many

relations, and as for friends, Charley says Papa was very quarrelsome and broke contact with all his friends. Debts, you know."

Ash nodded understandingly. He did indeed know. "So you're stuck with Cousin Albert?"

"Yes, and it's all legal," Toby agreed gloomily. "Charley checked with the solicitor."

Mr. and Mrs. Dyson did not readily welcome strangers to their farm, especially crumpled, muddy and unshaven ones, but once Ash produced several shining gold coins, they warmed right up.

They loaded Ash and Toby with produce; generous portions of home-cured bacon and ham, a couple of eggs—the hens didn't lay much during winter—two kinds of cheese, some root vegetables, a dozen apples, a little withered but still sweet and good, two loaves of fresh bread, a batch of ginger biscuits still warm from the oven, a pot of honey from their own hives, a small packet of tea from the farmer's own store, some sugar, a large jar of milk, and a bag of nuts. No coffee, which was a disappointment. Ash was very fond of coffee.

There was even a hare, skinned and dressed ready for the pot, and some winter greens. Toby turned his nose up at the greens, but Ash had developed a taste for vegetables in the east. And at the last minute, the farmer's wife had pressed on them a stoppered stone jar of warm soup and a generous slab of her own fruitcake, "A gift for you and the lad, sir, with our best wishes."

"It's like Christmas," Toby declared excitedly as they left laden with their treasure. The Dysons had provided them with a large wicker basket and a couple of hessian bags to carry all the food in.

*Christmas?* Ash blinked. He'd forgotten about Christmas. It wasn't long to go, a few weeks. He'd be long gone by then. He hoped.

He'd asked the Dysons about a doctor, telling the couple that the boy's sister had suffered a small accident. They'd shaken their heads gloomily. "Old Doctor Evans is mortal ill, sir. They're saying he's on his last legs—well, he's eighty-six. You might try willow bark tea," Mrs. Dyson added as she bustled about filling the basket with various goods. "That's good for pain. And fever."

On the way back to the cottage, Ash noticed the graceful shape of willows by a stream. Willow bark. What exactly did he do with it? He should have asked the farm woman, but they were almost back at the cottage and he didn't want to leave Charley alone any longer than he had to.

She'd been sleeping when they left, but he knew she'd be in pain when she awoke.

He set the basket and one of the bags down. "Wait here," he told Toby. "I'm just going to get some of that willow bark."

"For tea?" Toby wrinkled his nose. "It's very nasty."

"You've had it before?"

The boy nodded. "I was sick and Charley made me drink it. It was horrid."

"Good. I'm going to make some for her." Ash hurried across to the little grove of trees and took out his knife. Bark was the thing, but from the trunk or from a branch? He had no idea, so he cut some of each.

"Will it make her better?" Toby said when he returned.

"Let's hope so."

## Chapter Four

The first thing Charley was aware of when she woke was that her arm was on fire. It took a few moments until she could focus enough for her scattered memories to return. There had been a stranger, a man. He'd shot her. That explained the arm.

"Toby?"

No answer. She struggled up on one elbow, tried to pull the curtain aside and caused it to collapse instead. She glanced around the cottage. It was empty. "Toby?" she called again, this time louder.

A muffled quack from the box near the fire reassured her somewhat. Toby wouldn't leave Hannibelle, not for long.

Unless he had no choice. "Tobbbyyyyy!"

Silence. She struggled to sit up, but an unwary movement sent a sharp shaft of pain through her and caused her to fall back on the bed.

She lay quietly a moment, gathering her strength, then carefully sat up, shielding her injury, and swung her legs to the side of the bed. Cold stole over her—in more ways than one. Why was she only wearing her chemise? Since the cold weather had begun she always wore several layers of clothing to bed. Her bare skin prickled with cold.

Who had undressed her? Not Toby, that was certain.

A bandage covered the source of the pain. Neatly tied strips of white cotton. Toby hadn't tied that either. So where was the stranger? And where was her little brother?

She pulled the covers carefully around her. The cottage was chilly, but not as cold as it should be. The coals in the fireplace were still glowing. An all-night fire? They couldn't afford that.

She took a deep breath and tried to stand, but a wave of dizziness sent her back onto the bed. Her arm was the only part of her that was injured, but somehow, she was as weak as a kitten.

Voices outside alerted her, one deep and one high and excited. Toby. Relief rushed through her. She straightened, ignoring the pain and the dizziness, trying to look as if she was in command of her senses. She wanted the stranger gone. A glance at the window showed her the snow had stopped. Surely he could leave now?

She didn't like strangers knowing their business. Gossip travelled so easily. A chance word from one stranger to another could easily make its way back to Cousin Albert. And if he found them, all her efforts would be in vain and he would send Toby away.

The door opened, and Toby came in with a tall, handsome, elegantly dressed young man, carrying a large wicker basket and a sack over his shoulder. Toby was carrying another sack.

Seeing her Toby gave a shout of excitement. "Charley, look what we have! There's cake and biscuits and cheese and fresh bread and honey and ham and bacon and—"

Charley managed to stand. "Where have you been? I was so worr—" The words drained away and she swayed on her feet. The stranger swiftly dropped his burdens and swooped in and caught her before she fell.

"I'm all righ—" Strong arms lifted her and set her gently back on the bed.

"You should never have tried to get up," he said, straightening the tangled bedclothes out and tucking them around her. As if she were a baby.

She hated being so helpless, but she couldn't help it. Her head was swimming and her shoulder was aching

"How are you feeling?" he asked, and went on without waiting for her to respond, "The arm's hurting like the very devil, I expect, but any sign of fever?" He felt her forehead in a most familiar manner.

She tried to push his hand away. "We haven't even been introduced," she muttered, and then wondered why she was talking like a ninny. She'd tried to rob him. No introduction necessary.

"We have," he assured her. "You've forgotten—you were rather indisposed at the time. Blake Ashton, at your service, Miss Smith. Now, stay there and don't worry. You're a trifle feverish but Toby and I have everything under control, don't we Toby?"

Toby nodded, reassured by Blake Ashton's cheerfully decisive tone. "You should see what he bought from the Dyson farm, Charley. Fruit cake and bread and honey and biscuits and . . . " He chattered on, pulling things from his bag like a small triumphant magician, and setting them in a display around her on the bed.

She half listened to her little brother, enjoying his excitement—how long had it been since he'd sounded so happy?—but her dismay mounted with every item he produced. They couldn't possibly afford any of this, and she didn't want to be in debt to this man who was even now acting as if he owned the cottage and everything in it. Including her and her little brother.

Her life had been ruined enough by debt. And who knows what this man with the eyes that so unsettled her would want in return for all this treasure?

"We can't afford all this," she said dully, hating to ruin Toby's excitement. "You'll have to take it back."

"But Charley—"

"Nonsense," Blake Ashton said. He was doing something at the fire. Adding things to a pot. "Stop looking like that Toby, it's all staying here—until we eat it, of course."

"I can't afford—" Charley began.

"Nobody's asking you to." He carefully peeled slivers off a stick. "I bought it because there's not enough food here to feed a—" He glanced at the duck.

She stiffened, offended, even though it was true. But she was doing her best.

"Not enough food to feed an uninvited guest as well as you two," he amended. "Now stop arguing and tell me how much of this I need to put in water, and how much water for that matter. I presume you boil it." He took in her blank expression. "Willow bark. For the pain. Toby said you made it for him once."

"Yes and it's *very* nasty," Toby said with relish at the thought she was going to get a taste of her own medicine.

"Perhaps I'll make you drink it too," Blake Ashton said meditatively. "I hear willow bark tea is *very* good for growing boys, especially boys who talk too much."

Charley had to smile at the initial expression of horror on Toby's face, followed by laughter when he realized Blake Ashton was joking. Somehow the casual way he was teasing her brother made her relax a little. She lay back in the bed, and watched as he boiled up the willow bark, and at the same time made what appeared to be quite a competent stew in another pot, cutting a hare into chunks, and adding chopped onions, carrots and potatoes.

"Where did you learn to cook?" she asked after a while. She'd never known a man who could cook, not a gentleman, at any rate, and she was sure Mr. Blake Ashton was a gentleman. It wasn't only his very fine—though now rather grubby— clothes, and his clipped upper-class accent, it was his absolute assurance, his air of command—and his assumption of the right to command—even though it annoyed her.

He kept giving Toby orders, too—peel this, bring more water from the spring, fetch more wood for the fire. But somehow, the way he spoke to her brother was not so much man to servant, or even man to useless small boy, but more as if they were two gentlemen together, one tall and the other small.

And Toby was clearly relishing it. He happily ran and fetched and peeled, feeling important and needed. From time to time the man asked his opinion—usually about something small and insignificant, like whether to slice a carrot or chop it into chunks, or whether the fire needed more wood—but she could see that Toby liked being consulted.

His assumptions of how a gentleman behaved was bringing out the best in Toby; he was trying hard to please the tall man who had taken over their lives.

And though she had tried to rob him, and caused him to lose his horse, and even though he had every right to want revenge, or even justice, he was acting as if he had wholly dismissed the incident from his mind. And though it was probably foolish of her to believe him, she felt almost safe with him.

"Where did I learn to cook? Here and there. It's a useful skill." He picked up the pot of willow bark tea, swirled it around and sniffed. "How long does this need to steep?"

"At least half an hour."

"Does it really taste as vile as Toby says?"

She nodded. Right now she didn't care what it tasted like, as long as it helped with the fierce throbbing of her arm and the ache in her head.

He had unpacked the big basket and now he took down a small pot from the shelf where he'd placed it. "Honey might help with the taste." He tipped in a sinful amount of honey. Another argument in favor of his being a gentleman born—this man had never gone short in his life.

Even when Papa was alive, Charley had had to watch the housekeeping money like a hawk, though calling it the housekeeping money was a joke, really. Her father gave her no money for housekeeping or anything else. On the rare occasions he won, she'd steal as much of his winnings as she dared from him, to keep the household running. Then she'd hoard it like a miser because Papa would steal it back if he could, and gamble it away.

One by one the servants had left—even dear old Nanny McKeever had reluctantly said she could no longer stay without wages. "I've got my old age to think of, dearie," she'd told Charley sadly. She'd stayed long enough to teach Charley how to cook, taught her to make whatever food they had stretch, and to grow vegetables instead of flowers. Shopkeepers and farmers were reluctant to keep supplying goods to a household that didn't pay their bills.

It was an ugly and uncomfortable way to live. And then Papa had killed himself and Cousin Albert came into their lives and that was worse than ever. Until the only option left to them was to flee. And to try to make ends meet until she turned twenty-one.

Nanny McKeever's lessons had gone part way

to prepare her for this life, but it was harder than she'd expected when you had to do everything; provide a roof and warmth and food and clothing for herself and a growing boy. Plants didn't always grow, and even seeds cost money.

Another year before she turned twenty-one, and she would be free of Cousin Albert. She would be in charge of Toby then, and they could live on the money left to her in trust by her mother. The solicitor had assured her that though he'd tried, her father hadn't been able to touch that. It wasn't much, but now she knew the value of money, it felt like a fortune.

Another year. She wasn't nearly as sure of herself as she was when they'd started out. She wasn't even sure they'd be able to last through this winter. It had come unusually early and was much colder than anyone expected.

She needed to swallow her pride and be grateful to Blake Ashton for his gifts. And she was. But his apparent kindness worried her. Why would a stranger go to so much trouble for them? Obviously he felt responsible for her injury but after all, she'd been the one who held him up in the first place, so why would he stay? The snow had stopped earlier — though it was snowing again now. He could have walked to the road and sought help from passing travelers. Or borrowed a horse from the farm and gone on his way, instead of buying food for them all. Why stay here, where it was cold and uncomfortable?

And what repayment might a fine gentleman expect of a lone, unprotected female, after he'd spent so much money on them?

The fine gentleman cut some bread, buttered it and poured some steaming liquid into a bowl. "Sit up now. Mrs. Dyson sent you some soup and I think it will be better for you if you have something in your stomach before you drink this tea-stuff."

She shook her head. "Give the soup to Toby."

He snorted. "Toby, apart from his porridge this morning, has eaten a large vegetable pasty, two enormous slices of fruit cake, three warm ginger biscuits, numerous slices of bread and honey and who knows what else in Mrs. Dyson's kitchen. Add soup and the boy will burst. You, on the other hand have eaten nothing since yesterday." He bent over her and, without asking, he lifted her to a sitting position, and stuffed a pillow and the bed-curtains, which had fallen down again, behind her.

"Now . . . " He brought over the bowl, dipped a spoon in and proceeded to feed her like a baby.

"I'm perfectly capable—mmph." She swallowed.

"I know you are, but,"—he spooned another mouthful of admittedly delicious soup into her

—"you're still rather shaky and I wouldn't want you to spill this excellent soup in our bed."

"*Our* bed? mmmph." She swallowed and opened her mouth to put him straight on that. "It's not *our*—"

"Bread and butter?" He shoved a piece of fresh bread and butter into her mouth. "Good, isn't it?" he said as she ate it. "Now don't gulp it down. Wouldn't want you to choke. Here, have some more soup." The moment she swallowed the bread, he fed her more soup, preventing her from getting a word out. And the minute she swallowed that and opened her mouth to make it very clear it was not *his* bed in any way, shape or form, he shoved another bit of bread in.

Chewing, she glared at him. He grinned. "You have no idea how long it is since I've had good farm bread and good English butter. And the soup smells delicious, though of course we're keeping it all for you, being the invalid."

"I'm not an inval—mmmph."

"No, because I'm feeding you soup and building up your strength. Now stop arguing and drink this." He cupped the back of her head in one hand and held a cup to her mouth with the other.

*Stop arguing?* She hadn't been able to get a word out!

He tilted the cup and she had no option but to drink the nasty drink. Besides, she knew it would

help. She finished the cup, and shuddered reflex-
ively at the bitterness.

He frowned. "Not enough honey?" He reached
for the honey pot and seized a spoon.

She waved him away. "No, it's fine. Medicine is
meant to taste unpleasant."

"Nonsense, or why would there be honey in
the world? And we have plenty of honey, right
here."

"I don't want any honey," she said firmly. He'd
already used too much. She was grateful for the
food he'd brought them, but there were months of
winter yet to survive and every drop and crumb
counted.

He frowned, then shrugged. "Get some sleep
now." He removed the pillow from behind her
and settled her back down in the bed. He restrung
the curtains around the bed saying, "Now don't
fuss. Toby and I are going to play chess."

She frowned. "We don't have a chess set."

"We will improvise."

"But—"

"Sleep," he commanded, carefully closing the
bed curtains. "Knit up your ravel'd sleave of care."

It was irritating to be bossed around in her
own home—especially with quotations from
Shakespeare—but the soup and the bread and the
willow bark tea—and the honey—were making
her feel better, and the unaccustomed warmth of

the cottage was seeping into her bones. She must remember to tell him not to burn so much of their fuel . . .

*Chapter Five*

A chess set. It was all very well to say 'improvise' airily but it was quite another thing to do in a small, bare cottage surrounded by snow. Ash first thought of using nuts—hazelnuts or acorns—or even stones. But everything was buried under snow, and finding nuts would be almost impossible. There was no help for it but to carve the chess pieces.

He ventured out into the cold and cut some birch and willow twigs. The peeled bark from the willow twigs would differentiate them sufficiently. And the bark would be useful.

"You're really going to make a chess set?" Toby said as Ash sat down near the fire with his bundle of twigs and his knife.

"I'm going to try." He'd never carved anything, but he'd watched seamen carving scrimshaw. Not that he was trying for anything fancy.

He cut the pawns first, all roughly the same size, pointy heads for one team and square for the other. He whittled them quickly and gave them to Toby to smooth out with an old knife, and to scrape the bark from the willow team. The hardest part was making them stand up. Toby had great fun standing them up and watching them fall.

As they carved, they talked, softly so as not to disturb the sleeping girl.

"Papa had a chess set this big"—Toby showed the size with outstretched hands—"in ebony and ivory, but he had to sell it. The jade set also went. In that one the kings looked like Chinese emperors and the castles looked like a . . ." He frowned. "I've forgotten the name. Lots of curvy roofs going up in a kind of tower." He demonstrated with his hands.

"Pagoda?" Clearly it was a wealthy household. Again Ash wondered about the cousin.

Toby nodded. "That's it."

Ash had a similar set back home—in his most recent Asian house, anyway. Not that anywhere in particular was home anymore. He liked to move around. But his possessions usually came with him. There was a small exquisite carved jade traveling set in his baggage, in the boot of the hired chaise.

"You didn't have a traveling set?" he asked the boy.

"I did have," Toby said darkly. "A really nice little wooden one that came in its own box that you opened out and it was a chess board and you plugged the pieces into little holes so if the carriage bounced they didn't fall over. But it was in the bag that got stolen."

"You lost a bag?"

"No, it was *stolen*. When we were escaping from Cousin Albert. We didn't have much money, so we had to catch the stagecoach. I rode on the top. It was grand. But when we got off, we found that one of our bags was missing. Someone had stolen it."

Ash nodded. "There are thieves everywhere." He glanced at the sleeping alcove and hoped his erstwhile footpad hadn't heard his tactless remark. Luckily it went right over the boy's head.

They carved and scraped in companionable silence for a while, then Toby said wistfully, "I wish we were back at Old Place. All my things were there. But we can't live with Cousin Albert and Cousin Eustace Albert. They're mean." He heaved a sigh, scraped busily at a pawn, and then asked, "Where do you live, Mr. Ashton?"

Ash examined a bent, vaguely horse-shaped twig and thought about the question. Where did he live? "Oh, nowhere in particular."

Toby cocked his head curiously. "You mean you don't have a home at all? Are you a gypsy? You don't look like a gypsy."

Ash ran a rueful hand over his stubbled jaw. Without his shaving kit, he was probably starting to look like a gypsy. "I am in a way. I travel a lot, and I have a number of places where I stay, but I don't think of any particular place as 'home'." Not any more. He'd lost all right to a home ten years ago.

"Haven't you got a family?"

Ash hesitated. "No, I'm an orphan, like you." And didn't he feel guilty when he said that? He held up the horse-shaped twig. "Do you think this would make a good knight?"

Toby approved it, and they continued carving.

"Whereabouts do you travel to, Mr. Ashton? I've never been anywhere except here and Old Place. And London, but I was just a baby then and I don't remember."

"All over the world." But the boy wasn't satisfied with such a bare answer, and stories would help the time to pass, so Ash told him about some of his travels in the Far East and beyond—skipping over the circumstances in which he'd left England in the first place.

He told the boy about the exotic places he'd been to, weaving tales of the sort that a young boy might enjoy: tales of tropical islands with smiling golden skinned inhabitants who swam like fish and wore practically no clothes; other islands where the people were fierce and wore bones stuck through their noses—and practically no clothes; other hot places where the people wore so many clothes that they were covered from head to toe—all you could see were their eyes and their hands.

He talked about storms at sea, of encounters with pirates, of traveling in Chinese boats called junks, of playful dolphins, enormous whales and fierce sharks. He taught the boy how to greet people and to say please and thank you in several different languages.

He told him about places where monkeys swung from the trees, chattering and calling, where the birds were as colorful as a spilled paint box, and some of them could be taught to talk. He talked of the horsemen of Jaipur, and about the strange game men played on horseback in India and the far east, wielding long mallets in pursuit of a ball made of stuffed leather, but which legend suggested used to be made of the head of an enemy. Toby liked that tale especially.

In between stories Ash rose and checked on the girl. She slept on and off throughout the day, and when she woke, he fed her water and broth and willow-bark tea.

Finally, the chess pieces were finished and, after marking out a chess board on the battered old table—"Charley won't be happy about that, Mr. Ashton"— they began their first game.

Ash, who'd started the game with only half-hearted attention—after all, the boy was not yet ten—found himself on the verge of being soundly beaten. It took him all his wits to beat the situation back to a stalemate.

It was a shock. Ash almost never lost a game, and it was unthinkable to be beaten by a small boy. But the second game and the third proved that it was no fluke.

"I like playing chess with you, Mr. Ashton," Toby said at the end of the third game. They'd won one game each. "It's usually too easy to win, but you're really quite good."

"Glad to hear it," Ash said dryly. He understood now why Charley was so determined to send her brother to a good school. The boy was very, very clever.

In fact, now that he thought about it, young Toby reminded him of himself at that age. Ash had the kind of brain that loved to play with numbers and probability. And though that ability had made his present wealth possible, it had also been the cause of the worst action of his life . . .

He swallowed. He didn't want to think about that anymore. He'd done all he could do.

Toby began to set the chess set up for a fourth game. "Not now," Ash told him. "That stew should be ready in a few minutes. Go and see if your sister is awake—but don't wake her if she's sleeping."

He stirred the stew, and added some oatmeal to thicken it. Assuming Charley and her brother ever made it back to their rightful place in society, young Toby could be in exactly the same kind of danger that Ash had been—short on ready cash and high on brains, but not necessarily on wisdom. And, from all he could gather, without any kind of reliable steadying influence, other than his sister, to prevent him from making the kind of disastrous mistakes that Ash had made. And young men were rarely influenced by their sisters.

Perhaps Max would agree to keep an eye on the boy and his sister when Ash returned to the Far East.

"She's awake," Toby announced. "Is the stew ready? It smells deeeelicious." He inhaled with melodramatic ecstasy.

Ash chuckled. "Won't be long."

Charley was still very weak. That didn't surprise Ash because as far as he could tell she'd been on the verge of starvation for quite a while. She needed building up.

He brought her a bowl with chopped meat and vegetables floating in the liquid part of the stew. See if she could take that.

But before she would accept a mouthful, she struggled up on one elbow, and addressed her little brother. "Toby, are you all right?" In other words, did he feel safe with Ash?

Ash tried not to feel insulted; she didn't know him from Adam and he had, after all, shot her. But her suspicion, reasonable as it was, still rankled.

"Of course. We're going to play chess again later.

Mr. Ashton made us a set—see?" He held some of the chess pieces up to show her.

She nodded and subsided weakly. Ash propped her upright and when she indicated she would feed herself, he handed her the bowl, but her hand was shaking so badly he took it back and with a curt, "Be sensible now," he proceeded to feed her again. She managed to eat only half. He followed it with some more of the willow bark tea, and gave her a small piece of bread and honey to take the nasty taste away.

She ate only a mouthful and almost immediately drifted back to sleep.

Toby washed the dishes while Ash tidied up, and wondered how to pass the evening. It wasn't yet dark, so he glanced through the books on the shelf and decided to teach Toby some mathematics—though he disguised it as a game. As he thought, the boy was very clever.

Eventually though, darkness fell and, ridiculously early as it was, since he'd forgotten to buy candles from the farm, there was nothing to do except sit in the dark or go to bed. He took Toby to visit the outhouse and then, while the boy slipped into bed, Ash built up the fire and removed his boots and outer clothing. In drawers and shirt, he climbed over the boy and his sister and started to wriggle down in the bed between Charley and the wall.

"What are you—? Get out!" She thumped him weakly with her fist. "Don't you dare—"

He caught her fist in one hand. "Stop fighting me."

"I won't let—"

"This is where I slept last night. Did I harm you? Take advantage of you?" He wasn't going to tell her the state he'd woken up in. She didn't need to know that.

She didn't respond. Her eyes narrowed with suspicion and doubt.

"I am not sleeping on that cold stone floor. This way we will all stay warm." She continued to eye him with patent mistrust, so he added caustically, "And if you think I'd try to take advantage of you with your little brother sleeping in the same bed, you must have rocks in your head."

That seemed to get through to her. She didn't look any happier, but at least she didn't fight him as he slipped all the way into the bed. She turned her back on him and lay still, tense and rigid beside him.

Ash lay quietly, breathing deeply and evenly, feigning sleep, and he felt her body gradually soften against him. Her breathing slowed. She was asleep.

He, however, was wide awake.

The conundrum of her situation and what he could do about it kept battering at his brain. It was all very well to tell himself that she'd brought her injury on herself—had she held up someone else, they might simply have shot her and moved on, and Toby would have had to cope alone—but Ash couldn't shake the feeling of responsibility. And the more he got to know her and her brother, the more that feeling grew.

She hadn't brought her father's death or Cousin Albert and his horrid schemes on herself, and they were the crux of the problem. To be forced into marriage with a drooling simpleton or refuse and have her clever little brother sent off to a charity school with a reputation for cruelty—that was no choice at all.

And she and Toby were on the verge of starvation. They'd never last the winter out. Holding him up had been a desperate move. Courageous, too, if abominably risky.

He was a rich man. He could support them in comfort for the next five years, pay all Toby's school fees, even sponsor her for a London season without even noticing the expense.

But she was proud, as well as courageous. He doubted she'd accept his charity. She might, at a pinch, accept his paying Toby's school fees, but he'd bet his last penny that she wouldn't take a penny for herself.

She sighed in her sleep and turned toward him. Her breath was soft on his neck, her body warm and plaint. His body reacted predictably—well, dammit, she was a lovely young woman. He cursed silently and tried to will the sensations away. Without much success.

He tried to sleep. The problem of what to do about her churned around and around in his mind.

He was woken in the night by Charley moving restlessly and muttering. Ash felt her forehead. Hot and dry. Dammit.

He'd experienced fever many times in the Far East and had been treated with various Asiatic potions—none of which he had access to here—and soup, lots of soup. He remembered feeling as though he was burning up—or freezing. And always there was thirst, everlasting thirst.

He climbed carefully out of the bed.

"Whassa matter?" Toby mumbled sleepily.

"Nothing. Charley's a bit hot, that's all. I'll see to her. Go back to sleep."

"Orright." The boy was asleep in seconds. Ash ached for his innocence and the trust the boy had in him. He prayed it was warranted.

Dear lord, what if he'd killed her, this valiant, vulnerable young woman? He'd never be able to live with himself.

Before he'd gone to bed he'd placed the kettle on a hook over the fire, so it was still hot. He mixed some honey with hot water and added it to the willow-bark tea he'd made earlier. He lifted her a little, and fed it to her. It wasn't easy. She resisted, turning her head back and forth, muttering unintelligibly, but he managed to feed her what he hoped was enough for the moment.

Where the hell was a doctor when you needed one?

She was still burning up, so he put on his boots and went outside. It was snowing again, soft and steady. The night was strangely hushed. He wrapped several handfuls of snow in a rag, then pressed the cold pad gently over her body. It seemed to bring her some ease. He collected some icicles hanging from the roof and slipped them between her lips. That seemed to help, too.

An hour later she was shivering, and he built the fire up, and piled her with his coat and anything else that might warm her. The shivering worsened and he pulled her close, wrapping his body around her, belly to belly, chest to breast, holding her tight as he warmed her with his body-heat and willed her to live, to fight, to survive.

She'd slept a little then, and he did too, for about five minutes.

Some time later she was hot and thrashing around again, so he fetched more icicles and more snow. And fed her more willow-bark tea.

Later the chills started again . . .

And so it went through the night, until just before dawn. He must have slept, though it didn't

feel like it, because he woke with a start, knowing something had changed. She lay in his arms,
quite still, her breathing barely perceptible. Her
skin was damp. It took him a moment to realize it
was sweat; her fever had broken.

He sank back, weak with relief. It took him
several moments before he recalled that he was
wrapped around her in a more-than-intimate
fashion, their legs entwined, body pressed to body.
If she woke like that, any trust she had in him
would be shattered. He carefully eased himself
away, and felt instantly bereft.

He couldn't sleep now, and besides, just because
the fever had broken didn't mean she wouldn't
need further tending. He climbed out of the bed
and set about putting the cottage in order, building up the fire, brewing more willow-bark tea and
chopping wood.

## Chapter Six

Charley woke to the fragrance of bacon cooking. Dreaming again. These days she often dreamed of food . . . She closed her eyes and started to drift off again.

She'd drifted in and out of consciousness for most of yesterday. She remembered snatches of conversation between Toby and the man. Exotic places, adventures, animals. True or not? She didn't know. No doubt he just made them up to entertain Toby.

But real or not, they were revealing of the kind of man he was. So many of the stories were told in a wry, self-deprecating manner, not boastful at all, and some were quite definitely at his own expense. And told with dry humor than often made her smile.

Blake Ashton was kind to her little brother. Not many grown men would take the trouble. Or be so patient with Toby's endless questions. As for his care of her . . .

What was that? Hoofbeats? Her eyes flew open. It was no dream. She could definitely hear horses approaching the cottage. Nobody ever came down this track to the cottage. It was barely visible, even without the snow that would conceal the trail.

She tried to sit up, but a shock of pain stopped her. She'd forgotten her wound.

She heard voices—deep, male voices—and someone knocked on the door. Had Cousin Albert discovered them?

"Toby, make sure the door is barred and be as still as a mouse," she said urgently.

"Toby, open the door will you?" Blake Ashton said. "We have visitors and I don't want to burn this bacon."

Toby went running to the door. It was already barred, she could see. It must have been done the night before.

"No Toby!" Charley had to stop him. She got herself out of bed, took a few wavering steps toward the door, and reeled, suddenly dizzy.

Mr. Ashton swore, dropped the pan he was holding, and caught her up against his chest, just as Toby opened the door.

Cold air swept into the tiny cottage, and a tall, dark-haired man stood there, filling the doorway, a man Charley had never seen before.

For a moment, nobody spoke. Outside horses moved, harnesses jangled and men talked. Charley was breathless with fear.

The big man stamped his boots to free them of

snow, then stepped into the cottage. "Well, well, Ash, we came in search, half expecting to find you frozen on the side of the road. But here you are, fallen on your feet as usual, and with a beautiful young lady in your arms." His grin took in her, as well as Mr. Ashton.

"Max!"

Charley expected him to put her down to greet his friend, but instead his hold on her tightened. Two more men entered the cottage, stamping boots and brushing snow off their coats.

"So, you made it at last," a stocky man with an Irish accent said. "Better late than never, Ash, my wee lad."

"Wee? He's taller than you." Toby jumped in front of the Irishman and stood there, fists clenched, prepared to defend both Charley and Mr. Ashton.

The Irishman blinked down at Toby and chuckled. "Aye, he is at that, my brave young bantam, by a good inch or two, but I'm brawnier."

"It's all right, Toby," Blake Ashton said. "These are my friends."

Charley, aware that she was dressed in nothing but a crumpled chemise, and that the one called Max had glanced at her, taking in both her state of undress and her bandaged shoulder, pushed at Ash's chest. "Put me down."

He looked down at her as if he'd forgotten he

was carrying her, then nodded and set her care-fully down on the chair near the fireplace, where her bare feet could rest on the mat. He stood back, and was immediately surrounded by men, clapping him on the back and shaking hands and exclaiming over his arrival, and hurling questions at him.

"Toby, grab me a blanket," she hissed, and Toby ran to fetch one. She wrapped herself in it and felt slightly better for not being so scantily clad.

It felt like the little cottage was full of men, but in fact there were only four, including Mr. Ashton. It felt like more because they were all tall and well built—even the shortest of them, the Irishman, had to bend his head to enter the cottage—and it seemed they were all talking at once. They looked around the same age—thirty or younger—and all were warmly and elegantly dressed. And all were very handsome.

She felt like a ragamuffin in their company, clad in nothing but a patched and well-worn chemise and wrapped in a home-made blanket. And with her hair all over the place, straight out of bed. Not to mention the fact that would be obvious to all—that there was only one bed in the cottage. She knew the conclusion they would draw from that.

"Forgive us the invasion of your home, ma'am," the one called Max said to her, bowing in a courtly manner. "It's been a long time since we've seen

Ash here, and we feared he was dead. I am Max, Lord Davenham, and these are my friends and partners, Mr. Flynn and Mr. Monkton-Coombes." The three gentlemen bowed.

A lord? Charley felt scruffier than ever. She tried to smile, wondered if she could possibly stand, but before she could say anything, Toby stepped forward and bowed.

"Good day, gentlemen. I am Tobias Underw—"

"Toby!"

"Oh, yes, sorry." He gave the gentlemen a winning smile. "What I meant was, I'm Toby *Smith*, and my sister is Miss *Smith*." He bowed again.

Mr. Ashton's lips twitched. "Thank you, Toby, I should have introduced you all at the start." He slid a look of apology at Charley. "These gentlemen are my friends and business partners, Max and Flynn and Hyphe—er, Mr. Monkton-Coombes." He turned to his friend, the lord. "How on earth did you find me?"

"While Max is tellin' the tale, you won't mind if I just make a pot of tea, will you Miss Smith?" The Irishman added with a charming smile. "I can see you're in no state to play hostess to a rabble of unexpected guests."

Charley flung an agonized look at Ash. "I don't think we have any—"

"It's all right, Charley," Toby said happily. "Mr. Ashton bought tea yesterday at the farm. And there are some biscuits left. The cake is all gone, though."

Charley nodded, mortified at the exposure of their poverty. "Give the gentleman a hand, will you Toby? Nothing for me, thank you." She would love a cup of real tea, but there weren't enough cups. Bad enough that there were only two saucers, and one of them cracked.

"Max?" Ash prompted. "How did you find me?"

"Your carriage arrived this morning, empty but for your luggage, and the driver carried a message to say that the horse you'd hired returned to the stables two nights ago, with your saddlebags still buckled on it, and all your possessions still in them. Since no footpad would have left the contents undisturbed, it was obvious to us that you must have had an accident. So we set out to search for you."

"Expectin' to find you dead in a ditch, frozen solid," the Irishman interjected. "Would there be any sugar, Miss Smith?"

"No," she said. Her shoulder was throbbing painfully and she was starting to feel dizzy again.

"But there's honey," Toby said. "We got some at the farm yesterday."

"And that's where we got the first news of you," the man called Max continued smoothly. "They described someone who looked and sounded like you, but the boy with you was a surprise."

"Miss Smith and her brother are the reason I'm not frozen in a ditch," Ash said. "But they weren't expecting to have to cater for visitors."

He was lying. Lying to save her skin? Why? Because this lord might be a magistrate?

Charley's head started spinning. She needed to lie down. Urgently. She stood, shakily. "I think I'll just . . . " She wavered. Her legs crumpled beneath her, but before she hit the floor, she was caught against a firm, very familiar chest.

Ash tucked the girl back into bed. "Stay there," he told her when she struggled to rise, flinching as she bumped her shoulder. He fetched some more willow bark tea and fed it to her.

The cottage was silent. His friends were observing and no doubt coming to all kinds of conclusions.

"How was she injured? " Max asked.

"I shot her." Ash caught Toby's anguished expression, and added, "An accident, of course."

"Of course." From the look in Max's eye he knew Ash was lying.

Freddy Monkton-Coombes spoke up. "We brought a spare horse, but—"

Ash said curtly, "She can't ride in this condition. And I'm not leaving her."

"No-one is saying you should," Freddy said. "But you are definitely coming with us. The ladies are fretting."

"Only if Miss Smith and her brother come too," Ash said.

"I'm not going anywhere," Charley said.

Ash turned to his friend. "Max?" Max nodded.

Ash turned to Toby. "Toby, how would you like to come and stay with all of us for Christmas. It's warm and there will be people and games and toys, and mince pies and plum pudding and—"

"Plum pudding?" Toby's eyes were sparkling.

"Definitely, and sled rides, and all of these gentlemen play chess."

"All of them? Well?"

"Passably well."

Toby's eyes were shining. Charley's spat chips of ice at Ash. "You unprincipled, manipulative rat."

Ash inclined his head. "When needs must."

Freddy continued, "As I was going to say before I was interrupted, I'll ride back and bring the carriage. Easier for Miss Smith. And I'll bring Damaris who will know better than any of us how to treat her injury."

"Damaris?" Ash asked.

"My wife. Good with herbs and potions and things. More comfortable for Miss Smith to have a lady caring for her, too." Without waiting for Ash to respond, he left the cottage, closing the door carefully after him.

Flynn glanced around the cottage. "No place for a lone woman and child to spend a winter."

"I know that," Ash said irritably. "Why else do you think I stayed?"

"The wound?"

"Yes, but that's not the only reason." He didn't know what he was going to do. All he knew was that wound or not, he couldn't leave her and Toby in this situation.

"So what do you intend?" Max asked him with a silky undertone that Ash knew of old.

Ash frowned. He was perfectly aware of what it looked like, a cottage with one bed, her in the bed wearing just her chemise, him acting as if he belonged here. "I'm going to marry her of course."

"*What?*" Charley opened her mouth to object. Ash tipped it full of willowbark tea.

Max blinked. "Marry her?"

"It's the obvious solution," Ash said, as if he'd been planning it all along. The words had just popped out of his mouth, but now he thought of it, it was the perfect solution. He'd make a marriage of convenience with her. As her husband, he'd become Toby's guardian. And he'd support her and the boy in the manner they deserved.

"I'm not marrying you," Charley spluttered.

"Why not, Charley?" Toby asked. "Mr. Ashton is nice, much nicer than Cousin Eustace Albert, and he doesn't drool or anything!"

Max's lips twitched. "A noble endorsement."

"It's the obvious solution," Ash told her.

"No," she muttered. "It's out of the question."

Flynn brought over a cup of tea with a biscuit on the saucer, then glanced at her shoulder, handed her the cup and put the saucer with the biscuit beside her on the bed. "Here you are, Miss Smith, this'll help take that nasty taste out of your mouth." He added, "He's not much to look at, I know, but young Ash here isn't a bad catch. Honest, sober and very rich."

Charley glared at him. "You know perfectly well he's very handsome, but I don't care about that or anything else. I'm *not* marrying him." Her glance took in all of them as she added, "And I'll thank you all to stay out of my business."

The big Irishman gave a lugubrious sigh. "And there, I'm afraid, you'll be disappointed, lass. We're partners and friends, you see, and that means we're like family, and stick our noses in whether it's wanted or not."

Max nodded. "But if you really can't stomach marrying him, we'll think of something else."

"No we won't," Ash said. More and more he liked this idea. He could marry her, set her and Toby up in a comfort, make provision for anything they needed, and send Cousin Albert and his son packing.

She opened her mouth to argue, but Max interrupted. "Miss Smith needs to recover from her injury before coming to any decision about her future. Now, Miss Smith, in case you have any reservations, my wife and I would be delighted if you and young Toby here would join us for the Christmas festivities. Ash, will of course be joining us too."

"A Christmas party?" Toby exclaimed excitedly. "Oh Charley, a Christmas party!"

Clever clever Max, Ash thought. He was taking her to Max's anyway, but now it would be impossible for her to refuse without looking ungracious.

She frowned. Opened her mouth, closed it again. Then sighed. "Thank you, Lord um—"

"Max, please."

"Thank you, Max. That would be delightful," she said.

Ash hid a grin. She didn't sound in the least delighted. "Now you just lie there and rest and we'll pack for you," he told her. She gave him an agonized look. He knew she had very few possessions and that she was probably fretting about having nothing to wear. "Don't worry, it will all work out," he soothed.

She lay back looking anything but soothed.

With Toby's enthusiastic help, they packed up the books, the small valise of clothing, the home-made chess set—Max had told him he had several chess sets that he'd be welcome to use, but Toby insisted he wanted the ones that Ash had carved.

In a very short time all their possessions were

stacked in a small pile next to the door. It was rather a pathetic pile.

They heard the carriage pull up. "Anything else?" Max asked.

"Just that basket near the fire," Ash told him. "But be caref—"

The basket erupted with a loud Quack! and Max nearly dropped it. "What the—"

"Meet Hannibelle," Ash said.

"She's a duck," Toby said, and added a little anxiously. "A very special not-for-eating duck."

Max looked at the duck peering suspiciously out at him from under the piece of sacking. "A wild duck called Annabelle?"

"No, it's Hannibelle-with-an-aitch," Ash told him. "She's a very rare and precious Carthaginian duck."

"Of course she is."

The door flew opened and two ladies hurried in. "Oh you poor dear," the shorter one said. "Freddy told us about your accident, and you all alone here with only men to attend you. Never mind, we'll soon make you comfortable."

"My wife, Abby," Max murmured.

"And I am Damaris," said the other lady, slender and dark haired. "Are you in much pain, my dear?"

"No," Charley said.

"She is," Ash told them. "But she's being ridiculously brave and stubborn."

The ladies ignored him. They drew the bed curtains across, and the rest of the conversation was conducted in quiet murmurs. The men, knowing where their talents lay, loaded up the carriage.

After a few minutes, the curtains opened. Damaris said, "The wound seems to be healing, but Miss Smith is running a slight fever. We'll know more once we get to Davenham Hall."

Abby helped Charley to swing her legs out of the bed and wrapped her in the blankets.

"The carriage is very well sprung, but the road is bad and it's bound to be an uncomfortable trip. A few drops of laudanum will help you bear it." She smiled at Charley, and without waiting for her agreement, produced a small bottle, tipped two drops into the half cold cup of tea and handed it to her.

Charley grimaced but swallowed it down without argument.

"Now Max dear, if you will carry Miss Smith to the carriage."

"I'll carry her," Ash growled and carefully lifted Charley from the bed.

In a short time they had her comfortably stowed in the carriage, warmly wrapped and propped up between the two ladies. Toby sat opposite, Hannibelle in the basket at his feet.

At Charley's request, Ash, feeling strangely

redundant, securely locked the cottage—not that there was anything there anyone would want to steal. The carriage pulled away, the men mounted up and followed.

# Chapter Seven

The road was mired in melting snow and mud, and by the time they reached Davenham Hall, Charley was exhausted from the jolting of the carriage and the effort to be polite to these very kind ladies. She caught a glimpse of a sweeping drive lined with trees, a large, impressive house with columns and a tower and dozens of windows as the carriage pulled up. Servants ran out to meet them and, being deemed too weak to walk, she was swept inside in Ash's arms.

Under the supervision of the two ladies, he carried Charley up to a pretty bedchamber and laid her gently on the bed. He would have stayed to talk then—to argue about his ridiculous proposal of marriage, no doubt—but the two ladies had shooed him out.

"Now, my dear, would you like a hot bath?" Lady Davenham asked.

A hot bath. How long had it been? "I'd love one," Charley said. "You're very kind, Lady Davenham."

"Call me Abby. We're all friends here—more

than friends—we're like family."

The handsome Irishman had said much the same. Charley didn't understand, but she was tired and aching and she didn't have the energy to ask. The lady called Damaris disappeared and Abby supervised the footmen and maids who brought up pails of hot water and filled a large bath in front of a blazing fire.

Abby and one of the maids helped Charley to undress. She was mortified by the state of her worn, patched clothing, but Abby said, "Don't give it a thought, my dear. There's not one person here who doesn't understand poverty."

Charley gave her a skeptical glance. Poverty? Living in this luxurious mansion?

Abby smiled. "I know it doesn't look like it now—we've all been very lucky. But just a year ago Damaris and I and my sisters Jane and Daisy and even Lady Beatrice, who you'll meet in a day or so—they're traveling down from London— were in a desperate state. Without a home and on the verge of starvation—I promise you, it's true." She poured some creamy liquid into the bath and swished it around with her hand. The scent of roses drifted up with the steam. "Now, in you hop, Miss Smith."

"Please, call me Charlotte. Or Charley." She glanced at Abby and and decided she couldn't lie to her, not after her kindness. And if it was really true they were once homeless and destitute, well . . . surely she would understand. "And it's not really Smith, I'm Charlotte Underwood. I was—we were in hiding." She dropped the last of her clothes, and embarrassingly aware that she must look like a skinned rabbit, stepped into the steaming bath and sank down into the fragrant, steaming water. It was utter bliss.

Being careful not to touch her injury, Abby scrubbed her back while the maid washed her hair. Not since she was a little girl had Charley felt so pampered and cared for. She blinked back tears. After so long battling on her own, it was lovely to just let herself be looked after.

If she could, Charley would have stayed in that bath forever, but the water was cooling, so she stood and allowed the maid to rinse her down with several cans of clean hot water. Abby then wrapped her in large fluffy towels that had been heated in front of the fire.

A creamy flannel nightgown lay ready on the bed. "Oh, but I couldn't—" Charley began.

"It would please me if you accepted it, Charley," Abby said firmly. "A small Christmas gift."

Of course, Charley had no option then. She put it on and it felt so lovely against her skin—soft and warm with dozens of tiny mother-of-pearl buttons down the front. She climbed into bed and oh, it was so comfortable and the covers so warm and light. A goose-feather quilt.

Damaris came in then, carrying a covered tray. She smiled at Charley. "You look a bit better now. Isn't a bath the loveliest thing, especially when you're cold and tired and aching? Now, we won't keep you up for much longer, just to drink this soup. And I want to check your injury again, and then we'll leave you to sleep."

"Damaris is something of a healer and a cook as well," Abby explained. "Her soups kept us going when we were in the attic. She saved Jane's life." She took the bowl of soup from Damaris and began to feed Charley in such a matter-of-fact manner that Charley didn't like to insist on feeding herself. She felt ridiculously shaky and if she did try to drink the soup in bed she might spill it down this lovely nightgown and over this beautiful quilt.

"The attic?" Charley asked between mouthfuls. The soup was delicious.

"That time a year ago that I mentioned," Abby said. "Damaris, Jane, Daisy and I were destitute and living in the attic of a condemned building. Jane had a fever, and I thought she was going to die—Jane is my younger sister—but Damaris healed her."

Charley stared, wide eyed. Could it possibly be true? These charming, elegant ladies, destitute and living in the attic of a condemned building?

"Time for those stories later," Damaris interrupted. "Drink up your soup now, and I'll take a look at that wound."

She unbuttoned Charley's nightgown, and eased it carefully down to bare her wounded shoulder. "A little inflamed but it's healing," she murmured. "This will help." She took out a small pot of greenish paste and smeared it carefully over the wound. It was cold and smelled clean and pungent. She laid a square pad of gauze over it and bandaged it lightly. "Have you had any willow bark?"

"Mr. Ashton force-fed me gallons of it," Charley said wearily.

The ladies laughed. "Good for him. It will help," Damaris said. "I've made a little potion for you." She poured a spoonful and held it to Charley's mouth.

"Not laudanum—" Charley began.

"No, just some willow bark and a few other herbs and spices, with honey to make it palatable," Damaris told her and deftly slipped the spoonful between Charley's lips. It didn't taste too bad at all. "Take a few sips whenever your pain gets worse. Now, we'll leave you to sleep. Nothing is as healing as sleep."

"My brother—"

"Is currently downstairs beating my husband at chess" Damaris said. "After having delighted Cook by eating everything she put in front of him and telling her he'd never tasted anything so delicious but she must not even *think* of cooking his beloved duck. He's quite a character, isn't he? Don't worry about Toby, Charlotte, Blake Ashton is taking good care of him."

Charley smiled. "Mr. Ashton has been very kind, I suppose being an orphan too, he understands how Toby feels."

The two women exchanged glances. Charley was sure it carried some significance, but she was too tired to think. Damaris picked up the tray—the bath had been removed, and the room tidied while Charley was drinking soup and she hadn't even noticed—while Abby drew the curtains. Then they tip-toed out and closed the door.

Charley was feeling quite dazed. Just a handful of nights ago she'd been cold and hungry and desperate enough to turn footpad, and now here she was, warm, fed and safe, cocooned in absolute luxury. She snuggled down under the soft covers, closed her eyes and slept.

Ash came downstairs feeling like a new man after a bath, a shave and a complete change of clothes. Max's valet, Poole, had attended him, a man of quiet competence who'd shaved him like a dream. He followed Ash downstairs and waited quietly by the door.

A huge fire blazed in the hearth. Freddy Monkton-Coombes was sitting at a low table frowning over a chess board on which were arranged the rough wooden chessmen Ash had carved. Toby sat opposite.

Ash grinned. "Getting thrashed, are you?"

Freddy looked up and said with dignity, "I wasn't paying attention the first time."

Ash laughed. He glanced at Flynn and Max, who were observing. "You too?"

"I have several very fine chess sets, but he insists on using those dreadful pieces," Max said.

"They're not dreadful," Toby flashed. "Mr. Ashton made them for me. My traveling set was stolen, but I like these better—the pointy-heads and the blockheads."

Ash chuckled. "And which are you?"

"The winner." Toby moved a piece. "Checkmate, Mr. Monkton-Coombes."

Freddy spluttered and stared at the chessboard. "How the devil did you do that?"

Toby gave a grin that struggled not to be gleeful.

"Time for your bath now, Toby." Ash gestured toward the waiting valet. "Poole will take you up."

Toby gave Ash an aggrieved look. "A *bath?* But Charley already makes me wash every day. And you did too."

"Yes, in a small pot of water with a wash-cloth,"

Ash said firmly. "A bath washes the parts you can't reach. Off you go."

Toby sighed and reluctantly stood.

"Cook has a batch of her special shortbread in the oven," Max said casually. "It will be ready for Toby after his bath."

Toby brightened. "Shortbread? Oh, I do like shortbread. Thank you for the game, Mr. Monkton-Coombes. Perhaps we can play again," he said, and allowed himself to be escorted upstairs.

After he'd gone, Freddy said explosively, "What the devil is that child doing living in a freezing hovel? Manners like that, and a fine little brain."

Ash nodded. "I know. Send for coffee and I'll tell you what I know." Over coffee and a plate of gingernuts he explained about the shooting 'accident' and what he'd learned so far about Miss Charlotte 'Smith' and her brother.

"That's why I'm going to marry her," he finished. "As her husband I'll be able to send that villainous cousin of hers packing, along with his drooling son, and set her up in comfort and security. And as Toby's legal guardian I'll be able to see he gets the education he deserves."

There was a short silence, broken only by the sound of the crackling fire. "And then what?" Max asked.

Ash frowned. "What do you mean, 'then what'?"

Flynn leaned across and took a gingernut. "He

means, are you going to settle down in England and play happy families?"

Ash gave him a blank look. "No. I'll go on as usual, of course."

"Back to the Far East?"

"Yes, of course. Why not?" He had no intention of staying long in England. He'd get Charley and Toby settled and then be gone as quickly as possible.

The three other men exchanged looks. "If I've learned one thing so far in married life," Max said, "it's that women don't like it if you make decisions for them."

Freddy nodded. "Absolutely."

Flynn grinned. "The lass seems like a fine wee spitfire. It might be quite entertaining to watch her explain to Ash-lad the error of his thinking."

"Error of my thinking? What do you mean? It all makes perfect sense."

"Of course it does. To you." Flynn leaned across and stole another gingernut. "But then you're still running from the past, aren't you? I thought your comin' here might signal a change, but it hasn't."

Ash didn't answer. He finished his coffee, set up the chess-pieces and ate the last gingernut. It was none of Flynn's business anyway. And his plan to rescue Charlotte Underwood made perfect sense.

On Damaris's orders, Charley stayed in bed the following day as well. "Yes, I know it's 'just a bullet wound'," Damaris said when Charley protested, "but it and the fever have knocked you badly. No doubt your worries and an impoverished diet haven't helped. You need rest."

Charley had no answer for that. So she stayed in bed and did a lot of sleeping. Abby and Damaris and various maids bustled in and out, tending to her. In the evening she was feeling so much better, Toby was allowed to visit.

He sat on her bed, chattering happily, full of the delights of this new life, and how the men had gone out on horseback and Mr. Ashton had let Toby ride with him. "And this morning Lord Davenham found some sleds from when he was a boy and we all went out and sledded down the hill at the back of the house. And then we built a snowman, and then Mr. Ashton made a snowball and threw it at Mr. Monkton-Coombes and he threw one back and then they both threw one at Mr. Flynn and I threw one at Lord Davenham and we had the most splendid snowball fight, and oh, Charley, you should have been there, it was such fun."

And Cook was making him all his favorite things to eat, and lots of Christmas food, including a plum puddings the size of a cannonball, and mince pies and shortbread and all sorts of delicious things.

And Hannibelle? She was living in the poultry house and had made friends with another duck, and was well fed and safe from foxes.

Everyone was taking more of a benevolent interest in a small boy than Charley would have expected from a group of sophisticated people. And Toby was clearly flourishing, particularly under the masculine attention.

But how on earth were they to return to their life in the cottage now that they'd been showered with such kindness and attention? And food.

Nobody had mentioned Ash's ridiculous proposal of marriage. Thank goodness. Perhaps she'd imagined it. She'd been feverish at the time.

Later that afternoon Charley was sitting up in bed reading a novel when she heard a commotion downstairs, the sound of voices and laughter—particularly feminine laughter—and lots of coming and going of servants.

Fifteen minutes later she heard a voice outside her door say, "Well, let's meet this wounded gel of yours," and without further ado, an elegant old lady with improbably bright red hair entered her bedchamber leaning on a stick. She was followed by Abby and Damaris and two other young ladies, one blonde and very beautiful and the other short, dark haired, elfin-pretty and with a limp.

Charley sat up, putting her book aside.

"I hope you don't mind the interruption," Abby said with an apologetic look, "but Lady Beatrice and my sisters were anxious to meet you." It was clear from her expression that it was the old lady who'd instigated the impromptu visit.

She introduced the old lady as Beatrice, Lady Davenham—"Call me Lady Beatrice, my dear, everyone does." The other two were Jane and Daisy Chance, Abby's sisters though they didn't look much like her or Damaris.

To her surprise, Daisy the young lady with the limp, spoke with a broad Cockney accent. She eyed Charley, gave her a friendly smile, and with a "Back in a tick," she left the room.

They settled Lady Beatrice in a comfortable armchair and the other ladies found seats and settled down, clearly ready to chat. A few moments later servants arrived, bringing a large pot of tea, and a tray of elegant little sandwiches, dainty cream-filled cakes, an apple cake and some crisp almond biscuits.

A few moments later, Daisy came back. "Here you are, Miss Underwood, put that on." She passed Charley a gorgeous, hip-length jacket in soft rose pink, with ruffles down the front. Charley had never worn anything so pretty in her life. Or anything so expensive. And she didn't even know this girl.

"But this is silk," she began. "I couldn't possibly—"

"Nah, put it on. Think of it as a Christmas gift," Daisy said. "I'm a dressmaker and I make dozens of these. Good for when you're stuck in bed. Especially when you get unexpected visitors and want to look pretty." She inclined her head toward the old lady, currently investigating the little cream cakes, and winked.

"Yes, dear gel, put it on. Daisy has an eye for these things," Lady Beatrice said absently, without raising her eye from the cakes.

Abby and Damaris took the lovely garment from Charley and eased her into it, being careful of her injury. "There," Abby said. "Doesn't that look lovely?"

"It's beautiful," Charley said, stroking the silky fabric. "I can't thank you enough, Miss Chance." She was overwhelmed by the generosity of the gift.

"Call me Daisy. And it's my pleasure. I like to dress ladies up pretty. It's me special talent, according to Lady Bea here. This kind of thing was one of the first things I ever made her."

Jane came forward with the tray of delicacies, saying in a soft voice, "Can I tempt you with one of these delicious morsels, Miss Underwood? Or is there anything else you need? Another novel? Your pillows plumped up? Convalescence can be so tiring."

Charley thanked her and took a cream cake. Such kindness to a stranger.

By the end of the afternoon tea, all the young women were on first name terms and Lady Beatrice was beaming like a benevolent queen over her subjects. They told Charley a little of their history—the attic story amazed her—and introduced her to the concept of 'sisters of the heart' — sisters by choice, not by blood. It was a lovely idea.

"And she's going to be our sister too," Abby said, "because she's going to marry Mr. Ashton."

"No I'm not!" Charley said, cutting off the babble of congratulations.

"But I thought . . ." Abby began. "I'm sure Ash said—"

"He might have said it, but it's all his idea and I'm not having any part of it." She glanced around at the puzzled faces surrounding her and added, "He thinks he's being noble, but I have no intention of playing the beggar maid to his King Cophetua."

The old lady snorted. "Pish tosh! What nonsense! Beggar maid indeed! Anyone can tell you're a lady born."

"I'm sure he doesn't mean—" Abby began.

"He does," Charley insisted. She turned to Abby and Damaris. "You saw how Toby and I were living—they're just temporary difficulties—but Mr. Ashton has decided he will solve all my problems with a marriage of convenience. And besides, he didn't even ask me!"

Lady Beatrice sat up. "Didn't ask you? Pshaw! We can't have that, men just announcing things without so much as a by-your-leave."

Abby frowned. "Actually, Max told me that after the wedding Ash was planning to return to the Far East . . ."

Lady Beatrice snorted again. "And what's the gel supposed to do after the wedding when young Ashton swans off to the Far East, eh? Twiddle her thumbs? Faugh!"

"Exactly," Charley said, pleased to have someone who understood. She hadn't known about the plan to abandon her after the wedding, but now that she thought about it, it was implicit in what he'd said. Or rather, hadn't said.

She stifled a pang of hurt, telling herself she could possibly feel betrayed by the idea—she barely knew the man.

"Men are delightful creatures, but occasionally ridiculously thick-headed. Don't fret my dear, we'll soon sort this nonsense out." Lady Beatrice rose ponderously to her feet. Abby and Daisy hurried to help her. "And your husband will *not* abandon you."

"But that's not what I meant at all," Charley began, but the old lady had reached the door. Jane ran to open it.

"Delightful to meet you, dear gel," the old lady said over her shoulder. "But it was a long journey and I need a little nap before dinner."

## Chapter Eight

The next day Damaris gave it as her opinion that all danger of a relapse was past and Charley could come downstairs for a few hours. To Charley's embarrassment, Abby provided her with all new clothing, from the skin out, dismissing Charley's protests with a wave of her hand. "I have far more clothes than I need, and this dress will suit you better than it suits me. It will please Daisy, too, as she told me this fabric wasn't the right color for me, but it was so pretty I ignored her."

"Daisy?"

"She made it. She makes all our clothes. Talented isn't she? Now here's Sukey who will look after you. She will be your maid for all the time you are here."

A maid of her own? More and more Charley felt overwhelmed by the generosity of these people.

Sukey came in carrying a can of steaming water. She helped Charley wash and dress. The dress needed taking in but they made do with pins.

"I'm that pleased to be your maid, Miss," Sukey

said. "I've always wanted to be a lady's maid. Now, how about I braid your hair?" As she braided Charley's hair in a coronet around her head she chattered on, and the more she said the more dismayed Charley became.

More guests were expected—it was to be an extended family Christmas—the first Christmas at Davenham Hall for more than ten years, and Lord and Lady Davenham's first Christmas as a married couple. They were newlyweds, Sukey told her, as were Mr. and Mrs. Monkton-Coombes. And everyone on the estate was thrilled.

Sukey described the preparations going on downstairs, the geese that had been killed and were hanging in the cold room, the pig that had been slaughtered, the puddings that had been made, the sweets, the Christmas cakes . . .

But Charley wasn't listening. She and Toby were interlopers. They had no place in a family Christmas. They ought to leave. But how could they? Apart from the physical difficulty of leaving—it would have to be on foot and the weather was bitter—could she bear to drag Toby away from what was probably the best Christmas he'd ever had?

Not to mention the best one she'd ever had. Christmas at Old Place had always been tense, depending on Papa's mood, and whether Charley had been able to create a feast from the inadequate funds he'd allowed her.

"But it makes perfect sense," Ash said, exasperated. The girl was being ridiculously stubborn. She'd come downstairs earlier, looking pale and a little fragile, but still quite deliciously lovely—though he wasn't going there. He wanted no messy entanglements: it was a practical marriage of convenience he was proposing. Nice and straightforward. A business deal. More or less.

She'd thanked him politely and refused, just as politely. But Ash wasn't giving in that easily. "Marriage to me will free you from the control of your ghastly Cousin Albert and the threat of being forced to marry his horrid son. It will also save Toby from the horrors of the Grimswade school. Legally, I'd be Toby's guardian, but of course I'd leave the day-to-day decisions to you. I'll put his name down for my old school and—"

"No. I want him to go to Papa's old school—Eton."

"Which *is* my old school. Also Max's and Freddy's."

"Oh."

"And I will set you both up financially—"

A furrow appeared between her brows. "Why would you do such a thing?"

Ash had worked that out earlier. "Compensation for shooting you."

She scowled. "Don't be ridiculous. I held *you* up."

"But I wounded *you*, so no argument. I'll make you a regular allowance and I'll open an account for Toby—to pay for his school fees," he added as she opened her mouth to argue. "He's a very clever little boy and he deserves the very best education."

She considered it for a few moments then sighed. "Very well, if you wish to open a school account for Toby, I'll gladly accept it. And I will—reluctantly—accept a small sum of money as compensation for your shooting me. But I won't marry you."

"Why ever not?"

She tilted her head and gave him a searching look. "Why do you want to marry me?"

"Because it makes sense."

Her lips tightened. "And if we were married, what would we do?"

"I'd settle you both back in your rightful home, send Cousin Albert to the rightabout, organize your finances and fix everything else that needs to be done."

"And then?"

Ah, this was the tricky part. "And then we go on with our lives."

"With me at Old Place and you, where? The Far East? Having the kind of adventures you entertained Toby with?"

"What's wrong with that?"

"Nothing—for you. But what would I do?"

Ash didn't respond. How the devil did he know what she'd do? Whatever women usually did.

She continued, "Marriage is until death us do part. Under your arrangement, I'd live as a virtual spinster for the rest of my life, no children, no husband, no family."

"You'd be in control of your own life, and with no financial worries."

"Money." She dismissed it with a curt gesture. "I know what it's like to live alone, Mr. Ashton. It's *lonely*. I've been running my father's household since I was twelve. I'm almost twenty but I've never been out into society, never been to a dance or a party—only to church, sometimes. It's not how I want my future to be."

She rose awkwardly from her chair, wincing as the movement pulled on her injury. "So thank you kindly, Mr. Ashton. It's a generous offer but my answer is no. I don't want a bloodless convenient marriage—I want to live! I want children! I want to love and be loved! I want a family and friends."

Ash thought about it. "What if I gave you a child?"

Her eyes kindled with outrage. "What? Get me

with child and then go off and abandon me? Oh that's big of you!"

"That's not what I meant." It was exactly what he'd meant, but the way she put it, 'abandon' sounded ugly. He was thinking more like 'free.'

"No? Then what did you mean?" She waited a moment, then when he didn't answer, she said, "I thought so. Spare me your half-hearted charity, Mr. Ashton. I don't want a bar of it." She left the room, closing the door carefully behind her.

"So, how did it go with your young lady?" Flynn asked when Ash joined the men in the billiard room.

Ash snorted. "She's not my young lady."

"Is she not?" Flynn raised a brow.

"She won't have a bar of me. She told me so herself just now." And called him 'Mr. Ashton' as if he were a stranger.

"And what did you offer her?"

Ash glared at him. "Marriage, of course. And financial security for her and the boy. And freedom."

Max frowned. "Freedom?"

"Yes, freedom to go her own way after the marriage."

"So you're still planning to head off back to the Far East?" Max said in a voice that was far from approving. "Leaving her behind?"

"Yes." He'd make sure she was secure and well protected. It was more than she had at the moment. Her words echoed in his mind. *I want to live! I want children! I want to love and be loved! I want a family and friends.* He swallowed.

"And she didn't jump at such a princely offer? I'm amazed." Flynn shook his head. "So clever with numbers, so clueless with women."

Ash glared at him. It was a fine offer. Most women would jump at it. Just not Miss Charlotte Stubborn-is-my-middle-name Underwood.

"Well then, she's turned you down, so you'll not mind it if I ask the lass to marry me, then. She's a pretty wee thing, a real lady and that lad is a cracker."

"Just you damn well stay away from her!" Ash snapped. The strength of his reaction shocked him.

"Touchy, aren't we?" The laughter faded from Flynn's eyes. "She and the boy can't go on the way they were, Ash. Something has to be done."

"I know that," Ash snarled.

"Do you, now? Then do something about it." Flynn strolled out.

"Why are you so keen to marry her?" Max asked.

"Because I care what happens to her, of course. Did you not see the way she was living?"

Abby had just entered. "So it *is* King Cophetua

and the beggar maid."

"No it's not," Ash said, revolted. It was nothing like that at all.

"Sounds like it to me," Abby said. "And it's what Charlotte thinks, too—she said so. Max darling, could you come and help me with these decorations, please? I need someone tall." Max rose and they left the room.

Ash stood by the fireplace, and started gloomily into the flames. How could Charley think such a thing. She was no beggar maid, she was a . . . a prize. He'd never met anyone like her.

"The thing about women," Freddy said diffidently from his armchair, "is that they need to be wanted. They like to talk about *feelings*." He crossed one leg over the other and gazed thoughtfully at his boot. "Terrifying prospect, baring your soul, but there's no other way for it. I know it feels easier to avoid hard truths but . . . Faint heart never won fair maiden and all that."

After a short pause he glanced at Ash, "The boy mentioned that you'd told them you were an orphan."

Ash shrugged uncomfortably. "It seemed easier."

"See, that's what I'm saying. There's quite a bit you're avoiding, isn't there?" He held up his hands. "Not that I'm criticizing—Lord knows, I'm hardly the model to follow. Successfully avoided uncomfortable truths for years." He contemplated his boot again. "Took my wife to get me to open my eyes." He looked up at Ash and added, "And for what it's worth, the result is worth the pain. Like lancing a boil. Not that I've ever had a boil, but you take my meaning."

Charley took herself back up to her bedchamber. Her exchange with Ash had tired her, but it wasn't that so much as needing to be alone that took her there.

He'd missed the point of what she'd been trying to tell him. Her own fault. She'd been too indirect about some things, and at the same time too blunt about others. That ridiculously man-like oblivious notion of getting her with child before he sailed off into the sunset. How could he think that any woman would be content with that?

And how did you tell a man who loved his adventurous, exotic roving life that you wanted him to stay? Wanted to tie him down.

Hardest of all, how did you tell a man you'd known such a short time that you thought you'd fallen in love with him? When he gave no signs of feeling the same. And instead was full of plans to save her. And then leave her.

She didn't want saving—well, she did, but only from Cousin Albert's machinations, and not at the cost of her heart and the rest of her life. Cousin

Albert was a legal problem and all she had to do was avoid him and wait him out until she turned twenty-one.

She had more options now than when she and Toby had first stolen away in the night to board the stage and flee their home and Cousin Albert. She understood more about how difficult it was to support the two of them alone. But now, at Davenham Hall, she'd made friends, friends who might be able to help her keep Cousin Albert at arms' length and protect Toby, might be willing to help her find a better situation, as a governess, perhaps or a companion or maid. As long as she could keep Toby with her.

She thought about Ash's offer to pay for Toby's education. If it came to it, she supposed he could go to school, but she was reluctant to send him yet—he was such a happy and imaginative lit-tle boy and he'd have to fend for himself with all those much bigger boys at school, even if it was a good school. That's what they did at those places—made men of boys. She wasn't ready for Toby to be made a man of. Yet.

He'd flourished under the guidance and exam-ple of Ash and his friends, and was learning to be a man by copying them. That was enough for the moment. She'd send him off to school when he was twelve or so. Unless she had no other choice.

"Hey there, young man. I want a word with you."

Ash glanced around. It was Max's aunt, Lady Bea.

"Yes, you, young Ashton. Over here." She patted the seat beside her. "Come along, don't dally."

Amused by the imperious old thing, Ash joined her on the sofa.

"Now, about this young lady of yours, I have the solution to your problem."

Ash stiffened. He'd had enough of people telling him what to do. Bad enough the gratuitous advice from his long-time friends, but this old lady—she might be Max's beloved aunt, but that didn't give her the right to be poking her nose into his business.

And Charley was *not* a problem. Just her attitude.

"Excuse me—" he began and tried to rise, but she grabbed him by the sleeve and hung on like grim death. Apart from bodily dragging an old lady across the floor, Ash had no choice but to remain.

She chuckled. "Don't like being told what to do, eh? Like every other man. It's no use trying to escape, dear boy, because I'm an old woman and one of the privileges of age is to interfere and give unwanted advice. So just you sit here and listen to me.

"Now, as I understand it, you accidentally wounded young Charley, and stayed on to help her and her young brother—yes?" Without waiting for a response she continued. "That shows you have a good heart."

"I could hardly leave her bleeding in the road," Ash muttered.

"No, but you did a great deal more—including compromising her." Ash glared at her, but she said calmly, "One bed, wasn't it?"

"Shared with her little brother."

She waved a gnarled, heavily beringed hand. "Irrelevant. So, you wounded her, you compromised her, and you cared for her—I understand you tended her quite affectingly—and before you try to deny it, I got all this from the little boy. He's a clever little lad. Reminds me of Max at the same age."

Ash didn't respond. He was waiting for her to make her point or release his sleeve—whichever came first.

"I understand you offered for the gel because you pity her and her brother, and feel guilty that you injured her. And of course, because you compromised her."

Ash gritted his teeth and waited. She was completely mistaken. Pity had nothing to do with it. Guilt, only a little.

"But you don't need to marry the gel," she

continued. "I've taken a liking to her and the boy, and am willing to take them in. With Abby and Damaris off being married women, my house is denuded of nieces. The boy would help liven the place up and the gel could go about with Jane, and make her come-out. She's a pretty little thing; it won't be too hard to find her a suitable husband."

"She's going to marry me," Ash ground out. How many times did he have to say it?

The old lady produced a lorgnette from somewhere and directed it at him. "Because you pity her and feel guilty?"

"No, because—" He didn't know why, he just knew he had to marry her.

She waited, and after a moment repeated, "Because?"

Ash didn't answer. It was none of her business.

"Do you imagine young women dream of men who feel *obligated* to marry them?" she said caustically, and snorted. "Pity and guilt are poor reasons for marriage, young man. No gel of pride would take a man on those grounds—unless she was a gold-digger, and young Charlotte isn't, is she?"

No, she wasn't.

"So think about it, dear boy, and decide what you really want. You don't have to marry the gel to save her—if it's saving that's needed, I'll save her myself. But if you want her, you need to show her. A gel needs to be courted." She released his sleeve and smoothed it, then patted his arm, saying, "Now, off you run." Quite as if he was a schoolboy.

# Chapter Nine

Ash was sitting on Charley's bed playing cards. The door was wide open and a maid was hanging about in the corridor outside, pretending to polish the wood paneling—some kind of chaperone, he supposed.

He was in the middle of showing Charley a variation of Patience played with two people when she said abruptly, "Abby tells me you're not an orphan at all, that you have a mother and a sister living not far from here."

Ash fumbled his cards. Did nobody in this wretched house have nothing better to talk about than him and his situation?

"Why did you pretend they were dead? Was it pity for Toby and me? Because if it was—"

"It wasn't pity." Blast Max for blabbing to his wife. How much of Ash's story had he told her? And how much did Charley know?

"Then why did you lie to Toby and me?"

"Strictly speaking I only lied to Toby."

"And that makes it all right?"

He fiddled with the cards, straightening and

rearranging them, playing for time. She pushed them to one side. "Please don't ignore me," she said quietly.

"I'm not. It . . . it's complicated."

"Take as much time as you need." She folded her hands and waited.

Ash bit his lip. He didn't want to tell her, didn't want her to know the kind of man he really was. She seemed to imagine he was something of a hero, wrong as he knew that to be, and he was reluctant to disillusion her. "It's an ugly tale."

"You've heard my ugly tales."

He gave a mirthless laugh. "Your cousin is the ugly tale—you've behaved with honor and grace."

She snorted. "I tried to rob you."

"You had your reasons. I . . ." He ran his fingers through his hair. "There was no excuse for what I did."

"Tell me," she said softly.

Ash's jaw was tight. He hadn't spoken of this for years, had locked it away, tried to forget it. But if he wanted her to marry him—and he did—she needed to understand, needed to know what kind of man he was. He took a deep breath. "I gambled away my home and everything I owned and left my mother and my sister homeless and destitute." There it was, the bald, ugly truth of it.

There was a long silence. "When was this?"

"Ten years ago."

"So, you were what—eighteen?"

He nodded. "All through school I played cards and I always won. I have ... a facility with numbers, you see. We were, I suppose you would say poor, though we had a grand house and plenty of land surrounding it, but my father was a gambler, and there was never any money to spare. I supported myself through school on my winnings—that's another benefit of going to a good school; mixing with rich boys—and could sometimes send extra to my mother."

She nodded. "My father was a gambler, too— not a very good one."

"I was—I am—a good one. But I was young and arrogant and overconfident, and I didn't real-ize how badly drink—wine and brandy—would skew my judgment. I never much liked drinking and I wasn't used to it. But there I was, just eigh-teen, in a prestigious London club, invited to play with sophisticated gentlemen much older than I, offering me drinks, treating me as an equal ... I suppose I was flattered. And foolish. And cock-sure," he added bitterly.

"And so you lost everything."

"Yes, the house, the land—everything. Mama lost her home and my sister Louisa, who was betrothed, lost her fiancé—he reneged, the swine. Said the whole thing was a scandal and he wouldn't marry a pauper."

Her eyes were troubled. "What did they do?"

"Went to live with distant relatives. As poor relations. Living off their *charity*." He clenched his fist, feeling his nails bite into his skin. "They were evicted from the family home just before Christmas."

"Oh Ash." She placed her hand over his.

"I don't want your sympathy," he muttered. "I don't deserve it. It was my fault, all my fault."

She didn't remove her hand. "Yes it was, but you were a boy of eighteen. So what did you do then?"

"I ran away." Fled in shame and misery.

"Where to?"

"I didn't care where. I got on the first ship leaving England and worked my way across the ocean, ending up in the Far East. Where I attempted to drink myself to death."

"You failed at that, I see."

He shot her a glance. Was she laughing at him? No, but nor was she dripping with easy sympathy. It made it easier to go on.

"Max found me in a gutter in Batavia—we'd gone to school together, though how he recognized me, drunk, dirty and destitute as I was, I have no idea. He took me in, sobered me up and set me to work." And once he was himself again, Ash had found that the skills that made cards and chess so easy for him had proved even more useful in business.

"I haven't had a drink since then."

She nodded. "I remember you telling me."

"After several years I made enough money to buy back the family home. And make my mother an allowance."

"Good for you. So your mother is back in her home now? And your sister?"

"Mama is, but by then my sister was married. To a *grocer*." And didn't that mortify him? His sister selling soap and cabbages for a living when, before Ash had ruined her life, she'd been betrothed to a baron. From all he'd gathered she'd married the grocer shortly after the disaster. A desperate move to survive, perhaps. The thought flayed him.

"Is she happy?"

"How would I know?" He couldn't bear to think about it.

A faint frown marred her smooth brow. "Haven't you asked her?"

"No." He looked away. Her eyes were so damned clear he couldn't bear to look at them in case they showed what she thought of him.

"When did you last see your mother or your sister?"

There was a long silence. Ash gathered up the cards and shuffled them. She waited. The silence weighed more and more heavy. "Ten years," he muttered eventually.

"Ten years?" she exclaimed. "You haven't spoken to your mother or your sister since you left?"

"I send them money each month through our agent," he said hearing the defensiveness in his voice. "I've been in the Far East for the last ten years."

"And letters?"

His silence answered her.

"Oh, Ash." She reached out to touch him again, but he jerked his hand away. She gave him a thoughtful look. "But now you're back in England you'll visit them, of course."

"No I won't," he muttered. "What's the point? The damage is done. It's all too late." He slipped off the bed. "I warned you it was an ugly story. So now you know the kind of man I really am."

"But surely your mother will—"

But he was gone. "—have forgiven you by now," Charley said to the empty room.

*Now you know the kind of man I really am.*

Her view of Ash was so different from how he saw himself. Yes, he'd made a terrible mistake but he'd been just a boy, and the fault really belonged with those sophisticated older men who'd made a green boy drunk and callously stripped him of all he possessed, not the least of which was his self-respect.

And after his initial wallowing in remorse and self-disgust—which was understandable—Ash had made up for it as best he could, working hard to repurchase the estate and ensuring his family was safe again. No mean feat.

And yet he was still excoriated by guilt and shame.

His mother and his sister, how must they feel not having seen or heard from him for nearly ten years? Receiving an allowance instead, as if money were all that mattered.

If she'd been in their position and Toby had gambled everything away, she'd still want to see him again, to assure him she still loved him.

Surely Ash's mother still loved him. And was grieving for her son. You didn't raise a man to be kind to female footpads and small boys— and ducks—and not be able to forgive him for one boyhood mistake, however disastrous. Ash's mother would surely have forgiven him long ago.

But until he saw his mother again, he would never be able to forgive himself.

And that, she saw suddenly, was why he was so determined to return to the Far East. To continue his self-imposed penance, cut off from those he loved, hugging his shame to himself and living as an exile.

Oh, he could talk of adventures and the delights of exotic locations, but ten years and he still couldn't come home? Still couldn't visit his mother? It was a festering wound if ever Charley had seen one.

Telling Charley his sorry tale had been both harder and easier than Ash expected. Her response had given him much to think about. She hadn't seemed disgusted. Or even terribly shocked. Nor had she swamped him with easy, unconvincing sympathy.

And hearing himself relate the story after so many years . . . there was a distance to it that he hadn't been able to achieve before.

Needing to be alone, needing to think, Ash took a long, cold, reflective walk through the woods. The crunch of snow beneath his feet, the icy air that scoured his lungs with every breath, the still, silent forest—it helped clear his mind. He thought about all that had been said and done over the last few days.

By the time he returned to the house he was half frozen but felt somehow lighter and more energized. Being back in England—and it did feel like home, no matter what he'd been trying to tell himself—hearing what his friends had been telling him, and most of all, listening to what Charley Underwood had said—and more she hadn't said—he'd come to several painful realizations.

He'd been a craven coward. All these years telling himself he had a fine adventurous life—he'd been fooling himself. He'd been in hiding.

One thing was clear: he couldn't go on the way he was, not if he wanted to marry Charley Underwood. And he did, more than anything. And it wasn't from pity or charity or guilt or any other of the stupid reasons everyone was ascribing to him.

She'd come to mean so much more.

But she wouldn't marry him while he planned to return to the Far East, so something had to change. Someone. And it wasn't Charley.

Besides, he owed it to his mother and sister—and to himself—to face them.

As he entered the house he heard voices in the hallway: Toby and Charley. Their discussion was accompanied by odd clinking sounds. Curious, he peered around the corner.

"But I can't, Charley," Toby wailed. He was crouched at the foot of the stairs, collecting shards of what had once been a large china vase and placing them on a cloth. "What if they tell us to leave? And not stay for Christmas?"

"It's a risk you'll have to take," she said calmly. "But it would be a poor return for Lord and Lady Davenham's hospitality to lie to them, wouldn't it? Not to mention concealing your accident."

More clinking sounds. A short pause. "It might not be Lady Davenham's favorite vase. It was quite ugly."

"Does that really matter?"

"No," said a very small voice. Then he added hopefully, "But she might not notice it's missing."

"And what if she does?"

The little boy gathered the shards into a bundle and looked at his sister with a woebegone expression. "I'm going to have to tell her, aren't I, Charley?"

"Yes, love."

"Can I tell her later? Like tomorrow? Or maybe I could wait until after Christmas?"

Charley seemed to consider the suggestion. "It's up to you, of course, but in my experience the longer you put off something difficult, the harder it becomes to do it. And it might make your Christmas quite uncomfortable, hiding a guilty secret."

Ash strolled forward. "Your sister's right, Toby. If you explain to Lady Davenham that you didn't mean to smash her vase—"

"I didn't. I was sliding down the banister and I lost my balance."

"I'm sure she'll understand," Ash said. "And if you confess now, the hard part will be over and done with, and whatever she decides—no matter what the punishment—you'll know where you stand. And horrible possibilities won't be hanging over your head throughout Christmas."

"Do you really think it's best, Mr. Ashton?"

Ash nodded. "I know it is."

Toby heaved a sigh. "Very well then, I'll go and tell her now." Clutching the bundle to his chest he trudged away.

Charley turned to him with a raised brow. "Did I hear you correctly? You agree? That the longer you put off something difficult, the harder it becomes to do it?"

"Yes. I've been doing a lot of thinking."

"And?"

He cleared his throat. "If I went to see my mother, would you come with me?"

A smile lit her face. "Oh Ash, of course I will." She caught his hands in hers. "I'm so glad you're going to see her at last. I think you'll make this Christmas her best one in years."

Unconvinced, he grimaced. "And if she rails at me and refuses to forgive me, as she has the perfect right to do?"

"She won't, I know she won't. But if she does, I'll be there, right beside you." She squeezed his hands. "And whatever happens, you'll feel so much better for getting it off your chest at long last."

He wished he had her confidence. "It's a bit bigger than a shattered vase."

"I know. But to quote a wise man, it will be over and done with, and whatever she decides— no matter what the punishment—you'll know where you stand."

## Chapter Ten

They set out in Max's traveling carriage shortly after breakfast the following day. Ash hadn't been able to eat a thing. If he had, he would have lost it shortly afterward, he was sure.

He would have ridden by preference—it was only twenty miles—but after asking Charley to come with him, he could hardly leave her in the carriage to travel alone.

Conversation was sporadic—she tried for a time to keep him chatting about inconsequential things, but after a while she gave up, and started with the more personal, uncomfortable topics.

She asked him about his mother, and what sort of person she was. His answers were brief. He didn't want to think about his mother. Hard enough that he was going to have to face her.

She wanted to know about his sister Louisa, and the man she'd been betrothed to. The fellow was a lord and broke the betrothal after Ash gambled it all away, he didn't really know much more than that. He hadn't seen much of her in those last few years.

"She's my older sister. Most of the time I was away at school and she stayed with her godmother in London while she was making her come-out. Her godmother was sponsoring her, you understand." Because there was no money forthcoming from his father.

The miles crawled by. Despite the awkward conversation he was very glad to have Charley with him, her slight, warm body leaning against him, her arm linked through his. They'd found a large fur-lined rug folded on the seat, and he'd tucked it around them both, which made things warm and cozy—and took Ash's thoughts to the morning he'd woken with her in his arms.

Abby had offered to send a maid with them as chaperone, but Ash had claimed that there was no need. He'd already compromised her in the cottage, and if that didn't make her agree to marry him, nothing would. Besides, he didn't want any other witnesses to this meeting with his mother.

Finally they turned in between the high, wrought-iron gates of the estate. Everything looked neater and better kept than he'd ever seen it, the driveway raked, the garden neat, the hedges trimmed, his mother's beloved rose bushes pruned and awaiting spring in snow-covered, weed-free beds. The house, too seemed in good trim, the paint on the front door and the window frames no longer peeling, but crisp and fresh; everything neat and well maintained.

The money he'd sent had been put to good use.

And then they were pulling up at the front door. A groom ran up, pulled open the carriage door and let down the steps. Ash took a deep breath, and stepped out. He turned to help Charley down. She looked entrancing in a pale green wool dress, a dark green spencer, and a close-fitting bonnet that framed her face perfectly. She carried a woolen cloak over her arm—she hadn't needed it in the carriage. Her eyes were bright, and as she took his hand she gave him a warm smile that did a little to soften the cold hard panic that had seized him.

A butler answered the door, a man Ash didn't recognize. "Good morning, sir, madam, may I be of assistance?"

"Is Mrs. Ashton at home?" he asked.

The butler glanced from Ash, to Charley and then at the traveling carriage with the crest on it. "I will ascertain whether she is at home, sir. Please come in and wait."

Damn. Ash had forgotten the notion of people being at home, or not at home, depending on whether they wanted to receive visitors. Charley nudged him. "Tell him who you are," she murmured, but he shook his head. He didn't want to announce himself, not to this bland-faced individual.

He wanted his arrival to be a surprise. He wanted to see his mother's true reaction, not some prepared response she would display if she were forewarned.

They waited in the vestibule. A decade since he'd been here last. Ash wasn't sure if it was disconcerting or comforting. Everything looked the same—the same inlaid wood flooring, the same paneling, the same painting of a stag at bay—he'd never liked that painting. He liked it even less now. He knew how the poor beast felt, only the hounds that snapped around Ash were all in his head.

He took a few steps in one direction, then another, then stopped, trying not to pace. His throat was dry, his palms damp. He glanced at Charley, sitting tranquilly on a bench, looking around her with bright interest, and his heart swelled.

What a blessing his encounter with this sweet-faced, courageous, desperate young woman was. She'd been battling against impossible odds, and her courage had caused him to look past his fears, realize the self-deception he'd been practicing all these years, and to decide to face up to what he had done. She glanced up at him at that moment, and smiled.

He knew now what he wanted out of life.

"Blake?" An uncertain voice came from the stairs. He looked up. "Is it—can it really be you?"

His mother stood stock still for a moment, then came rushing down the stairs. She stumbled in her haste and Ash leaped forward and caught her.

She clung to him, tears running down her cheeks. "Oh Blake, my dearest boy! You've come home at last. Thank God, thank God."

Ash held her tight, breathing in her particular scent, a scent he didn't even realize he knew, so familiar and dear. "Mama." It was all he could say. A thick lump in his throat prevented him saying anything else.

His mother leaned back a little and gazed up at him, scrutinizing him, patting his cheeks, running her hands over his shoulders, smoothing back his hair as she used to when he was a boy. "You've changed. You're so thin, so brown, but oh, oh, you're home, you're home."

"Blake?" said a voice behind his mother. Ash looked up and saw his sister standing on the stairs. Behind her stood a tall, grave-looking man and two small boys. She wasn't smiling, wasn't rushing to embrace him. He braced himself.

"Louisa," he said.

His mother released him and, wiping her eyes, turned toward Louisa. "Look Louisa, isn't this the most wonderful Christmas surprise?"

Louisa came slowly down the stairs and crossed the floor to stand before him.

She stared at him for the longest moment. He

had no idea what she was thinking. She hit him hard on the shoulder. "Ten years," she said. "Ten years, Blake! We didn't know if you were alive or dead!"

"But I sent money."

"Money!" She hit him again. "As if that's all that mattered."

He stared at her, dumbfounded. What else had he failed to do?

"You still don't understand anything, do you?" she said, her voice breaking. Her eyes filled with tears. "It's you we care about, you big idiot, not your stupid money." She grabbed him and hugged him tightly.

When she released him, she gestured to the man on the stairs. "And this is my husband, Michael Gordon."

The cabbage-seller. Ash gave him a curt nod. "Gordon." Gordon returned it with equal reserve.

"And our sons, Peter and Phillip." Louisa beckoned and the two small boys came bouncing down the stairs. "Say good-day to your Uncle Blake, boys."

The two boys bowed and chorused as one, "How do you do, Uncle Blake?" Their bright eyes surveyed him speculatively.

*Uncle Blake?* He was an uncle? "Twins?" he asked his sister.

"Yes, eight-and-a-half years old."

He frowned. Eight-and-a-half years? He glanced at the grocer, but Louisa answered the question in his mind. "Michael and I married a few months after . . . " She glanced at the boys. "After, you know."

Gordon came forward and slipped his arm around Louisa's waist. "I met your sister at the circulating library. We found we had a lot in common." He smiled down at her, and Louise smiled back at him with such a look in her eyes, Ash was shocked.

"But I thought . . ." He'd always assumed she'd married the cabbage-seller out of desperation.

"Blake dear, who is this young lady sitting so quietly and patiently?" His mother approached Charley, saying, "Welcome to Ashton Manor, my dear. Is it you I have to thank for bringing my son home at last?"

"No, no, " Charley responded. "I just accompanied him."

"Mama, Louisa, this is Miss Charlotte Underwood, and yes, Mama, she may deny it, but she gave me the courage I needed to face you all at last."

His mother broke convention by hugging Charley, then she turned to her son indignantly. "Courage, Blake? To come home to your family? What nonsense."

Ash said slowly, "After what I did to you, I didn't

think I deserved a family any more. I'm so sorry, Mama, Louisa. I tried to make it up to you, but—" His voice cracked.

"Let us not discuss it here in the hallway," his sister said briskly. "Tea and biscuits in the drawing room if you please, Cotton. Miss Underwood, would you like to refresh yourself after your long trip? Boys, run along upstairs."

"Oh, but Mama, we wanted to ask Uncle Blake about his adventures in the Far East—"

"And whether he fought any pirates and did he see lions and tigers and—"

"Upstairs," their father said firmly. "You'll see your uncle at dinner."

"Dinner?" Dinner meant staying the night. Ash hadn't even considered the possibility. He hadn't thought past the initial meeting. "I'm sorry, I hadn't planned on staying the night."

"You're not staying?" Ash's mother exclaimed in dismay. "But surely after all this time . . ."

"It's my fault," Charley said quickly. "We weren't sure you'd be home, and I promised my little brother I'd be back tonight. He's almost nine, and I've raised him since our mother died when he was born. We've never been separated. Both he and Abby expect me back tonight."

Ash gave her a grateful look. "I can come back for a longer stay later, Mama."

"Well, if you're not staying to dinner I'll make

sure luncheon is a small celebration," his mother said, and bustled away.

"Michael, will you see to Blake? Come along Miss Underwood." Louisa swept Charley away.

Ash blinked. His sister had always been bossy. And she didn't seem the slightest bit crushed by her marriage to the grocer.

"If you'd like to freshen up ..." Louisa's husband indicated the way to Ash.

"I know where it is." Ash was still uncertain about this man. "I grew up here."

"Yes, of course."

"Do you live here now?" Ash asked.

"No, I have my own house a few miles down the road, but Louisa drops in on your mother most days." He glanced at Ash. "Your sister and I made a love match, you know. I can see you don't think I'm good enough for her, but she's a damned sight better off with me than she would have been if she'd married that lord she was betrothed to before." His voice hardened. "And after the mess you made of things ten years ago, you're hardly in a position to act all head-of-the-family now."

It was straight speaking of the sort Ash understood and it caused him to look at Michael Gordon with dawning respect. "I know," he said. "I'm sorry, I'm just a bit on edge."

"Expected to be hauled over the coals ten years after the fact, eh?"

"Something like that."

Gordon gave an ironic huff of laughter. "And instead you're getting the fatted calf." They reached their destination. "Well, here we are. I'll see you downstairs shortly."

Ash's sister showed Charley to a very modern *cabinet de toilette*. Charley used the facilities, washed her face and hands and tidied her hair, then prepared herself for an interrogation.

"Was Mama right, Miss Underwood?" Louisa asked the moment Charley emerged. "Are you responsible for bringing my brother home?"

"No, Ash—Mr. Ashton," Charley corrected herself, "brought himself here. I only came for . . . for the company."

"What are you to my brother, Miss Underwood?"

"A friend."

Louisa Gordon arched an eyebrow. "I see. And this 'Abby' you spoke of?"

"Another friend," Charley said coolly. She had no intention of explaining anything to this blunt-spoken woman. Ash's friends were for him to talk about, or not.

Louisa laughed. "Oh dear, now I've offended you. Mama will scold me. She's all ready to love you for bringing my brother home." She paused, then went on in a different tone of voice, "The thing is, Mama has grieved terribly for Ash these long years. I don't think my brother realizes how hard it has been for her."

"He realizes," Charley said. "And I believe he feels it very deeply. He's just not very good at showing his feelings."

Louisa gave her a thoughtful look. "You care about him."

Charley didn't answer.

"I do love my brother—I just don't want him breezing in here like a returning hero, getting Mama all stirred up and then disappearing for another ten years."

Charley could understand that. All the time Ash had been away it was Louisa who had cared for her mother, so her concern—and her bluntness— were understandable. "I cannot speak to your brother's plans," she said. "But I have every faith in his good intentions. Now, shall we go downstairs?"

## Chapter Eleven

"I'm so sorry, Mama, Louisa. I have no excuse for my actions. I was arrogant, cocksure and drunk, and I treated your home and your security with appalling carelessness. To lose so much in a card game . . . " Ash shook his head, still unable to accept the enormity of his action.

"Oh, but you were just—" his mother began.

Ash held up his hand to stop her. "Please, Mama, let me finish." He didn't want easy forgiveness, he wanted—he *needed* to explain, to take responsibility, and to apologize. Nothing less would do.

"I then compounded my dereliction with a despicable act of cowardice, running away to the other side of the world." He traced the carving on the arm of his chair, unable to meet his mother's eyes and continued in a low voice. "I was so ashamed, I wanted to die"—his mother made a distressed sound and clapped her hand over her mouth—"but I didn't even have the courage to do that." He closed his eyes briefly, remembering the depths to which he'd sunk.

"What happened?" Louisa asked after a moment.

"Max happened." He glanced at his mother. "Remember Max Davenham from school? He was a few years older than me, but—"

"I remember him," his mother said. "Max has been very good to me."

Ash raised his head in surprise. "Max has?"

"He wrote to me all those years ago—just after he ran into you in Batavia—to tell me you were alive and in good hands." She glanced at her daughter. "Until then, we feared you were dead."

Another wave of shame flooded Ash. He'd been so mired in self-pity and shame at the time, it hadn't occurred to him to write to reassure them. He'd assumed they'd prefer him to be dead.

"Max assured me he would look after you, and said he was putting you to work."

Louisa added, "And shortly after that, your first payment arrived."

There was a short silence. It all sounded so simple, but it wasn't. He was about to explain in more depth, but Charley nudged him under the table. He glanced at her and she shook her head slightly. He realized then that describing the depths to which he'd sunk would only add to his mother's distress.

Louisa's husband spoke up then, "I know this is none of my business but I have to say, you did amazingly well to have bought back the estate and returned your mother and sister to the position they'd held before."

"Not quite," Ash muttered.

"Blake Ashton, don't you dare bring up the name of that selfish beast I was betrothed to!" Louisa snapped. "His lordship dumping me was the best thing that happened to me. Granted, I didn't think so at the time, but believe you me, my eyes were opened to the kind of man he really was, once he thought my family was penniless. I am grateful to have been spared what I now know would have been an unhappy marriage."

She turned to her husband and Ash was stunned at the glow he could see in his pragmatic, bossy sister's eyes. "And then I met my beloved Michael, who saw only me, not my family name or estate or fortune—or lack of it. He didn't care about any of that." She stretched her hand across to him, and he took it and squeezed it.

"And you saw only me," Michael said. "And not my grocery stores."

"Grocery stores?" Ash blurted it out. Plural?

His brother-in-law said dryly, "You assumed, I suppose, that I ran the village shop, selling soap and potatoes."

Ash said nothing. It was exactly what he'd thought.

Louisa said proudly, "Michael owns—what is it now, my dear?—a dozen large stores in all the main towns."

"Something like that," her husband said in a way that made Ash certain that he owned a great deal more. He glanced at Ash. "I suppose you don't approve of your sister marrying a man in trade."

"Don't you dare look down your nose—" Louisa began fiercely.

Ash held up his hand, laughing ruefully. "Calm down, firebrand. As a man whose entire fortune comes from trade, I could hardly object. Not only have I spent the past ten years in trade, I am a senior partner in a major international trading company—Flynn & Co.."

Michael raised his brows. "I've done business with Flynn and Co.. A fellow called Bartlett."

Ash nodded. "Our head man in London, now also a minor partner in the firm."

"Well." The two men looked at each other with new eyes.

"So it might have started as a disaster," Louisa finished, "but for Michael and me it had a very happy ending."

"And for me," Ash's mother said. "Because I gained two beautiful grandsons as well as a wonderful son-in-law." She turned to Ash. "It was a dreadful shock at the time, of course, but it wasn't losing the house or the estate or the money that was so devastating, but the loss of you, my darling boy. The most important thing in my life is my family, and now, here you are returned to us, and back where you belong." She rose tearfully from her seat and embraced him again.

"I'm so sorry, Mama," he mumbled in her ear.

"Oh hush," she said, smoothing back his hair. "You've always been the best of sons—don't think I've forgotten how you used to send me money all those years when you were just a schoolboy. Now, you made one mistake—admittedly a big one—but whatever harm was done, you've more than made up for, and you've punished yourself enough. It's all in the past now, and I won't hear another word about it." She gave him another hug, then stepped back, saying briskly, "Now, it's almost time for luncheon, and I hope you don't mind, but I'd like the boys to join us and begin to get to know their uncle."

"They are convinced you're full of tales of adventure," Louisa said.

"He is," Charley said. "He's kept my little brother and me entertained with them for hours."

Ash blinked. He hadn't realized she been awake when he and Toby were talking.

"Yes, and now," his mother turned to Charley, "I want to know about you, my dear. You've sat here so quietly while we talked about all our family business, and I know you keep saying you're not responsible for bringing my son back to me, but I don't think that's entirely true."

"It's not," Ash said before Charley could respond.

"She gave me the courage to face my past, and to face you so I could apologize in person."

"I see." His mother and Louisa exchanged speculative glances.

"And she didn't come just for the company," Ash added. "I brought her to meet you because—"

"Because Lord and Lady Davenham asked me to convey to you this invitation," Charley said hurriedly, cutting off what she suspected might be another announcement of their impending—and imaginary—marriage by Ash.

He hadn't actually asked her. Or been given her reply. And she wasn't going to let anyone *assume* her into marriage. She gave Ash a sharp look and he grinned, unrepentant, but didn't continue.

From her reticule Charley produced a sealed letter and handed it to Mrs. Ashton. "Lord and Lady Davenham?" the older lady repeated, puzzled.

"Max and his wife, Abby," Ash explained. "Max inherited the title some years ago."

Mrs. Ashton read the letter. "Oh, how lovely, Max's wife has invited us all to Davenham Hall for Christmas. She said all the family, so do you suppose she means Louisa, Michael and the boys as well?"

"Yes, she told me to tell you there was plenty of room and she would love to be surrounded by family over the Christmas season," Charley said.

"Abby is an orphan," Ash explained. "It's her and Max's first Christmas as a married couple, and they've invited everyone they consider family."

Charley added, "She and Max have a very flexible definition of family—Max's business partners are included, and Abby's sisters—though only one of them is her actual sister—as well as Max's aunt, Lady Beatrice, who claims all the girls as nieces. They even include me and my little brother, and they've only known us for a very short time."

Louisa and her husband exchanged glances. "I'm not sure . . ." Louisa began.

"My brother would love the company of your boys," Charley told Louisa. "Toby hasn't had boys his own age to play with in ages. It would make his Christmas perfect."

"Yes, do come," Ash added, looking straight at Michael. "You'd be very welcome."

Mrs. Ashton was beaming. "That's settled then. We shall all spend Christmas at Davenham Hall. I must say I'm looking forward to meeting Max again after all these years. And his wife sounds delightful."

Over a large and delicious luncheon they made plans. Charley and Ash would return to Davenham Hall that afternoon, and Mrs. Ashton, Louisa, Michael and the boys would follow in two days time, after they'd packed and made their arrangements.

They set out for Davenham Hall late in the afternoon. It would be dark before they reached their destination, but the carriage had lamps, and they were in no particular hurry. Ash's family gathered on the steps of Ashton Manor, giving them the kind of farewell more appropriate for an upcoming two year absence, instead of a two day one.

Ash's mother really wanted him to stay. Charley felt a little bit guilty.

"Do you mind that I said we needed to return to Max and Abby's today?" she asked him as the carriage turned onto the road. She'd only said it because she thought he needed to escape.

"Lord, no. I love my mother and sister dearly, but this situation . . ." With a gusty sigh he leaned back against the squabs. "I'm exhausted, and yet all I've done is talk and eat."

"Emotions can be exhausting," Charley agreed. "Especially difficult ones." She was very glad she'd gone with him now, not so much because he'd needed her support—he didn't. He'd handled it so well.

But having observed him in his interactions with his family, she now understood so much more about him. The knowledge that he'd tried to support his mother even as a schoolboy, his protective initial wariness towards the stranger his sister had married, and his acceptance once he realized they were in love. His patience and kindness toward his ebullient young nephews—it was all adding to the image of Blake Ashton she had in her heart.

Because he was in her heart, she admitted to herself.

He had set such high standards for himself that he'd believed that his one terrible mistake was utterly inexcusable, that he deserved to live in exile, shunned and reviled by his family, that his mother and sister would never be willing or able to forgive him, no matter what he did to make up for it.

His helpless bewilderment in the face of their love and forgiveness had touched her deeply. He had no idea what a wonderful man he truly was.

"You were happy with how it went, weren't you?" she asked. He'd been staring out of the window at the passing scenery, a faint frown on his face. But he was so much more relaxed than he had been that morning. As if a weight had lifted.

He thought for a moment, then nodded. "Yes, except for one part."

Charley turned to him in surprise. "Which part was that?"

"The part where you interrupted me."

"I interrupted you? When?" She couldn't recall any interruption. For the most part she'd tried to be quiet and unobtrusive.

"When you stole my 'because' and substituted it with Abby's letter."

"Oh." Charley didn't know what to say. She'd cut him off deliberately.

"Yes, oh." For a long moment he said nothing, just gazed at her. "Do you want to hear what I was going to say?"

"Not if you're going to tell me again that you're willing to marry me and leave me at Old Place with Toby while you go off to foreign parts and have adventures."

"Why would I make such a stupid suggestion?"

She frowned. "You've made it before—several times."

"I must have been mad. Out of my senses. I was held up by a footpad, you know. It obviously scrambled my brains." In the gloom of the carriage his eyes glinted.

She eyed him warily. "All right, what were you going to say?"

"Correct me if I'm wrong, but today you seemed under the impression I wanted you with me to give me the courage I needed to face up to my past."

She shook her head, ready to refute his so-called lack of courage but before she could speak he continued, "That's partly true, but only a small part. The main reason was that I wanted you to meet my family at the most difficult possible time. And to see me with them."

"Why?"

"So that you could see them—and me—at our potential worst."

"Worst? There was no worst, potential or otherwise. I thought your family was lovely." He had no idea how lucky he was. People who had family so often took it for granted.

"Good, because I want you to become part of it." Before she could say anything, he swept on. "I've made so many mistakes in my life, and had many adventures, but the best thing that ever happened to me was when a small, gallant footpad held me up."

He took her hands in his and held them against his chest. "I don't deserve you, and knowing what you know, you might not want to depend on me for anything important, but if you could take a chance on me, Charley, I promise you I wouldn't let you down."

Her eyes sheened with tears.

His hold on her tightened. "I was lying when I said I'd leave you. I could never leave you." His eyes darkened. "I love you, Charlotte Underwood, with all my heart, and I want to marry you, and make love to you, and be a family with you, and have adventures with you."

For a moment Charley couldn't speak, her heart

was so full.

"So, will you marry me?" he asked.

She nodded. "I love you too, Ash. I have for the longest time." She leaned forward to press a kiss on him, but missed his mouth because of the jolting of the carriage. With a smile he gathered her gently against him, careful of her healing wound, and brushed his mouth over hers, so light and tender.

She sighed with pleasure and his hold on her tightened. He kissed her again, his lips firm and warm. Charley pressed closer, loving the taste and feel of him, the faint masculine fragrance of his cologne and the scent of . . . of him, so familiar and beloved from those nights in the cottage. They hadn't been dreams, she realized, and neither was this. Only a dream come true.

She pulled her gloves off and smoothed her palms up over his jaw, enjoying the faint prickle of bristles under smooth, masculine skin. He made a sound deep in his throat, and suddenly his mouth was all heat and hunger. She reacted instinctively, opening her mouth to him, pressing herself against him, feeling her insides heat and melt as she slid her fingers into his hair to cup his head and hold him close.

She lost all track of time, all awareness of anything other than Ash, as he lavished her with kisses, soothing the yearning ache of loneliness that had been part of her for so long. And she lavished him right back with all the love in her heart . . .

"For the longest time?" he asked some time later, when they were nestled together under the fur rug. "You've only known me a handful of days."

"Sometimes that's all it takes to know a person." She snuggled closer. "You could have left me bleeding in the road, but you didn't. You could have left Toby and me to struggle on by ourselves. You didn't. You could have been bored by and impatient with a small boy who gets underfoot, asking endless questions. You weren't. You told him stories and made him feel important and valued. You even made him a chess set, and respected his duck. And when I was ill you cared for me with such tender devotion . . ." Her voice broke.

He stared at her. "Are you sure it's me you're talking about?"

"Oh hush. You've allowed one great mistake when you were young to color a false image of yourself. You present yourself as reckless and rootless, but you're kind and protective and—"

"That's enough. I'll start blushing if you keep on with this nonsense." He drew her onto his lap and resumed kissing her. Charley had no objection to that at all.

# Chapter Twelve

In the lead-up to Christmas Day, Davenham Hall filled with people, all connected in some way; some cautiously feeling their way, others joyful in their reunion with long-lost family members.

It snowed again just after Ash's family arrived, and the world was white with pillowy, powdery snow. Naturally the three little boys were the first ones outside, building snowmen and racing down the hill on sleds, shrieking with excitement. The big boys soon followed, and then the women, and once the first snowball was thrown, a snowball war was on for one and all.

Afterward, pink-cheeked, pink-nosed and tingling deliciously from the cold, they all trooped inside for hot soup, eggnog or spicy mulled wine—or coffee in Ash's case. They ate hot sausage rolls, stuffed roasted apples, mince pies and gingerbread.

Fires blazed in all the main rooms. Nobody would ever be cold in Davenham House. They roasted chestnuts over the coals and baked potatoes in the ashes. They toasted crumpets and muffins, and ate them slathered with butter and honey or jam.

In the evening, as the fire crackled and the flames danced and wove shadows on the walls, they told stories of exotic places and thrilling adventures; of pirates and tigers and elephants and maharajahs and more. Cross-legged by the hearth, the three little boys listened, wide-eyed and enthralled. The various relatives were also fascinated.

They also played games; hunt the slipper, cards, blind-man's bluff, hide and seek, knucklebones, charades, as well as the more grown-up games of piquet and whist—and chess. On some evenings there was music, singing carols and other songs around the pianoforte, while some ladies sewed, and others cut Christmas ornaments from gold and silver paper. It was so lovely and peaceful at those moments, with the hush of the cold winters night outside and the beauty of the music inside.

Charley was floating on air. Ash had obtained a special license and they were to be married midway between Christmas and New Year in Davenham Hall's tiny ancient chapel.

Daisy had designed her a dress in a beautiful creamy fabric, warm and soft, and she and Jane and Charley were all working together, sewing it. As they sewed, and talked and laughed, they shared their personal stories and a hint of their dreams.

Charley was learning what it might be like to have sisters. Sisters-of-the-heart—it was a lovely idea.

Daisy had also made her a gorgeous dark red spencer in silk velvet—a gift from Lady Beatrice. It was so soft and lush Charley kept stroking it like a cat, until, "Oy! Stop that, or you'll have the bloomin' thing go bald before you get to the altar," Daisy said, laughing.

It truly felt like the gathering of one big, noisy, happy family. Several times a day Toby confided to Charley that he was having the best Christmas ever. He and Louisa's twin boys had become an inseparable threesome, and they dashed around madly, playing little-boy games and laughing like loons. And haunting the kitchens to beg treats from Cook, and because it was Christmas, the treats kept coming.

But despite all the exciting distractions, Toby didn't forget his Hannibelle, and went out to the poultry shed every morning and evening to make sure his duck was well fed and happy. Charley was so proud of him.

Christmas Eve dawned fine and sunny, and they all went out gathering greenery—boughs of fresh, sharp pine, sprays of red-berried holly, swags of ivy, and branches of fragrant bay and laurel. And of course, there was mistletoe.

With Max and Abby celebrating their first Christmas together, Freddy and Damaris still effectively on their honeymoon, and Charley and Ash about to get married, there was particular interest in the mistletoe. By the time the house had been decorated, there were sprays of mistletoe hanging in every room, at intervals along each hallway, and in every conceivable place mistletoe could possibly be hung.

"I'm never going to get married," Toby informed Charley that night when she tucked him into bed as usual.

"Why not?"

"Because at Christmas you have to kiss ladies all day! There's no time for anything else."

Christmas Day began with a trip to church. Snow squeaked and scrunched underfoot as Charley and Ash walked arm in arm, along with Max and Abby, Freddy and Damaris and Louisa and Michael. Flynn walked with Jane on one arm and Daisy on the other. Ahead, three small boys ran and jumped and gloried in the snow and the excitement of Christmas day.

The closer they got to the church the more people they met going in the same direction, and the air was filled with joyous seasonal greetings and an occasional spontaneous outbreak of Christmas carols.

Lady Beatrice and the older members of the

group arrived swathed in furs, riding in a horse-drawn sleigh. Heaven knew where Max had found it but it lent an added festive air to the whole proceeding.

Afterward it was back to the house and a magnificent Christmas feast—roast goose, venison, and all the works, finishing with the *pièce de resistance*, the biggest plum pudding Toby had ever seen, flaming with burning brandy and flanked by jugs of hot custard, thick cream and brandy sauce. Cook and the rest of the kitchen servants had outdone themselves. Everyone ate until they were full, and perhaps even a little bit more than full.

The day passed in a blur for Charley. All she could think about was that in three days time, she was going to be married. Her dress was finished, and they were working on several more dresses. And Daisy had presented her with the most beautiful nightgown for her wedding night — another gift from Lady Bea and the Chance sisters. "Not that I'll expect you'll be wearin' it for long," Daisy had added with a wink.

Boxing Day passed in a blink. Some went out in the early morning to watch the local hunt gathering, noisy with their horns and barking hounds and hallooing, and bright against the pristine snow in their scarlet coats—which for some reason that Charley didn't understand were called pink. The servants all received their Christmas boxes and went off for their own Christmas celebrations.

Charley barely noticed a thing. It was over-whelming—wonderful, but overwhelming. Just a few weeks before she'd been facing the worst Christmas imaginable, desperate, freezing with cold and on the verge of starvation. Now she had more than any girl could wish for, a group of people who'd drawn her and Toby into their family—and a darling man who loved her.

But there was one last dark cloud hanging over her. She needed to start her new life with a clean slate. She needed to tell Ash's mother the truth; what she had done, and how they had met.

On Boxing Day afternoon, when the house was quiet, she approached Mrs. Ashton and asked if they could talk in private. They found a small unoccupied sitting room, and sat down. Charley's hands knotted nervously. She couldn't think where or how to begin.

How hard it must have been for Ash to face his mother after what he'd done.

Mrs. Ashton reached over and placed her hand over Charley's trembling fingers. "What is it my dear? Surely it can't be as bad as all that?"

Charley took a deep breath and blurted it all out. "It's not the romance you think it is. Your son met me on the road when I tried to hold him up and rob him. I had a gun." Once she'd started it all came tumbling out; how desperate she'd been, why she and Toby had been hiding, and how Toby had thrown stones at Ash's horse and his gun had gone off and Ash had accidentally shot her. And how Ash had stayed and cared for her, how he'd looked after her and Toby.

Mrs. Ashton waited until Charley finished her confession. Then she rose and embraced Charley, being very careful of her injured shoulder, saying, "You poor dear, what a dreadful time you've had. Thank goodness Blake came along when he did."

Charley stared at her. "But I held up your son. I'm a footpad."

Mrs. Ashton laughed. "Don't be silly. You were desperate and you did a very brave—if foolish—thing for a very understandable reason. I'm only glad my son came along when he did." She hugged Charley again. "And you know, my dear, I think shooting you was the saving of my son. It woke him up to what is truly important in life. And I know you're going to make me a perfectly delightful daughter-in-law. Now, have you thought about what you're going to do for the honeymoon? Or where you're going to live?"

Charley hadn't. She didn't care about any of that. Ash had already had his lawyer write to Cousin Albert, informing him of Charley's imminent marriage, and pointing out that Cousin Albert would therefore no longer be Toby's guardian, and adding in strong legal terms that he and his son should immediately vacate Old Place and never darken its doors again.

The honeymoon she was leaving up to Ash.

"What are you doing with Toby during the honeymoon?" Mrs. Ashton asked. "You won't want a small boy tagging along, will you? Why don't you leave him with me, and I'll have Louisa's twins come to stay. The boys will be delighted, I'll have three grandsons to spoil and Louisa and Michael can have a little holiday."

It was the last weight lifted. Charley was no longer the sole person responsible for Toby's safety and welfare. She had family now who would help and support them both. Charley was free now, free to love and be loved.

Ash's wedding day dawned cold and gray with a sky of polished pewter. He dressed with a feeling of unreality. Just months ago he'd imagined he'd never see England again, never see his mother or his sister. He never expected to marry, thought of himself as a rolling stone, gathering no moss, no permanent home, no commitments outside his business ones.

Now . . .

He swallowed the lump in his throat. He adjusted his neck-cloth and stared at his reflection in the looking glass.

Now his world had a new axis to spin on, a new center of gravity—Charley Underwood, small, beautiful, and indomitable. And his.

In two more hours . . .

The Davenham Hall chapel was small and simple, just bare white walls with a few brass plaques, stone floors, and dark wooden beams overhead, but the windows were a glory of stained and colored glass, and the simply carved pews had been polished by generations of sitting bottoms, augmented with lashings of beeswax and elbow grease.

Ash waited in the front of the altar with Max, his best man, trying to tamp down his impatience.

Bunches of green pine and holly were tied to the end of each pew with red and white ribbons, scenting the air and mingling with the fragrance of beeswax polish. And something else, an aroma that was somehow familiar . . . and yet somehow exotic. It teased Ash's nostrils but he was unable to place it.

The small church was filling up, mainly just the guests from the Hall, and a few locals. On one side of the aisle sat his comrades of the past ten years. There was Flynn, sitting with Lady Beatrice on one side of him, and Daisy and Jane on the other. Next to them was Freddy with his lovely wife Damaris. A family of sorts, that had somehow swelled to embrace him and Charley and young Toby.

On the other side of the aisle sat Mama with Louisa and Michael with their two boys, well scrubbed and fidgety in their best clothes. Mama sat with a handkerchief clutched in her hand, her eyes already shiny with tears—happy tears.

So many blessings to be thankful for; friendship, family, acceptance, forgiveness.

He breathed in deeply to steady his nerves and suddenly recognized the scent that had so tantalized him. Joss sticks. He looked around and saw them burning at each corner of the church, not the usual English church incense, but redolent of the many temples of the Far East, where joss sticks were lit for luck, and to bring blessings and good wishes for the future.

The melange of fragrances in the ancient church was perfect, symbolic of the bringing together of the various parts of his life, the English, the Oriental, the past and the future.

There was a stirring at the entrance of the church and Ash turned, and there she was, his unexpected gift, the love of his life, standing straight and slender in the doorway while Abby, her matron of honor, fussed around her.

Dressed in a simple cream dress with a long-sleeved spencer in crimson velvet, Charley looked down the aisle at him and smiled. His breath caught in his throat. It was as if a candle lit her from within.

He wasn't sure what he'd done to deserve his luck, and this woman, but he was going to do everything in his power to make her happy.

She walked down the aisle on her little brother's arm, Toby so solemn and earnest in his new clothes, giving his sister away. To Ash.

Charley held out her hand to him. Ash took it and together they turned toward the altar.

The minister began, "Dearly beloved, we are gathered here today . . . "

Thank you for reading *The Christmas Bride,* my first independently published story. I hope you enjoyed it. Reviews help other readers find my books, so I really appreciate all reviews and ratings, whether positive or not.

If you'd like to read the other books in the *CHANCE SISTERS series,* you can buy them here:

*THE DEVIL RIDERS* — about men who are back from the war and finding it tough.

*The Stolen Princess*
*His Captive Lady*
*To Catch a Bride*
*The Accidental Wedding*
*Bride By Mistake*

I have also written two other Christmas novellas in anthologies with my fellow word wenches, and published by Kensington.

'The Mistletoe Bride' is in the anthology *Mischief and Mistletoe*

'Mistletoe Kisses' is in *The Last Chance Christmas Ball*

*Would you like to know when my next book is available?* You can sign up for my newsletter and/or blog at www.annegracie.com

Follow me on twitter: @AnneGracie

Like my Facebook Page:
facebook.com/annegracieauthor
Follow me on Amazon or Book Bub
and you'll be notified when my next
book is about to come out.

# About Anne Gracie

Anne Gracie spent her childhood and youth on the move, thanks to her father's job which took them around the world. The roving life taught her that humor and love are universal languages and that favorite books can take you home, wherever you are.

Anne started her first novel while backpacking solo around the world, writing by hand in notebooks. Published by Harlequin, Berkley USA and Penguin Australia, her regency-era romances are national bestsellers in the USA, have won many awards, been translated into more than eighteen languages and include Japanese manga editions (which she thinks is very cool). A lifelong advocate of universal literacy, Anne also writes books for adults just learning to read.

CPSIA information can be obtained
at www.ICGtesting.com
Printed in the USA
LVHW022308230423
745151LV00013B/680

9 780645 015119